GEEK GIRLS Don't CRY

GEEK GIRLS Don't CRY

Real-Life Lessons From Fictional Female Characters

ANDREA TOWERS

STERLING
New York

STERLING
New York

An Imprint of Sterling Publishing Co., Inc.
1166 Avenue of the Americas
New York, NY 10036

ISBN 978-1-4549-3339-7

Library of Congress Cataloging-in-Publication Data
Names: Towers, Andrea, author.
Title: Geek girls don't cry : real-life lessons from fictional female characters / Andrea Towers.
Description: New York : Sterling, [2019] | Includes bibliographical references and index.
Identifiers: LCCN 2018049212 (print) | LCCN 2018050723 (ebook) | ISBN 9781454933403 (epub) |
ISBN 9781454933397 (hardcover : alk. paper)
Subjects: LCSH: Women—Psychology. | Women heroes. | Women heroes in literature. | Courage. |
Conduct of life. | Feminism.
Classification: LCC HQ1206 (ebook) | LCC HQ1206 .T69 2019 (print) | DDC 305.4—dc23
LC record available at https://lccn.loc.gov/2018049212

Distributed in Canada by Sterling Publishing Co., Inc.
c/o Canadian Manda Group, 664 Annette Street
Toronto, Ontario M6S 2C8, Canada
Distributed in the United Kingdom by GMC Distribution Services
Castle Place, 166 High Street, Lewes, East Sussex BN7 1XU, England
Distributed in Australia by NewSouth Books
University of New South Wales, Sydney, NSW 2052, Australia

For information about custom editions, special sales, and premium and corporate purchases,
please contact Sterling Special Sales at 800-805-5489 or specialsales@sterlingpublishing.com.

Manufactured in the United States of America

2 4 6 8 10 9 7 5 3 1

sterlingpublishing.com

Cover Illustration by Paulina Ganucheau
Interior design by Shannon Nicole Plunkett
Cover design by David Ter-Avanesyan

Images Credits: © Paulina Ganucheau (stars illustrations); iStock: © bonezboyz (female
superheros), © Tatiana Mezhenina (burst and dots); Shutterstock: © Kapitosh (speech bubbles),
© K1r1 (gradient dots), © Vitya_M (social media icons)

Dedicated to my family—
my own real-life heroes—with love

To *mom*, who gave me a cape and wings
and pushed me to fly;

To *dad*, who showed me the power of finding
your heroes on a screen or in a song;

To *Rebecca*, who has the greatest superpower of all:
being my sister.

CONTENTS

FOREWORD
IN THE COMPANY OF BADASS WOMEN
By Marisha Ray

For as long as I can remember, whenever I proudly brag about the women that I'm so lucky to have around me, I always end on the same boastful statement: "I only keep badass women in my life." Of course, that doesn't narrow down the candidates much, does it? Every woman is her own unique variety of fighter. This perception was always my brand of veneration toward our global sisterhood. The more that time passes, the more I realize that from struggle comes wisdom, and I haven't met a single woman that isn't a sage in her own way and doesn't have a message in the story of their lives.

From the moms we call "Wonder Women," giving a moniker to their strength and compassion, to the brilliant young women paving the way in traditionally male dominated fields with a tenacity and resolve reminiscent of Princess Leia, these fictional heroines give us tangible lexicons of comparison to the people we're surrounded by. As a fellow Geek Girl, whenever I'm reading a fantasy novel or watching a Marvel® summer blockbuster, the magnanimous virtues and qualities of these fictional characters always manifests the image of a loved one in the back of my head. Not only are we inspired by the strength and empathy of these pop culture icons, but they also highlight the heroes we have standing next to us.

Now, for me to limit these incredible stories and characters to mere tools of comparison would be a huge disservice on many levels. I've been an actor and producer in the entertainment industry for nearly fifteen years now. Over the course of that time, I've had many discussions on storytelling with numerous creatives, ranging from comic book writers to Hollywood directors. A common theme often presents itself: inspiration demands fuel, and as they say in *the biz*, "Write what you know."

As trite as the old adage may be that "art imitates life" and vice versa, it's deeply true. When you see Katniss Everdeen overcome tyranny or watch Jessica Jones struggle with guilt, that's the result of inspiration from a myriad of creators' personal influences. What these fictional conflicts tell us is a culmination of the best (and sometimes worst) parts of the human experience. How could you not feel emboldened by Storm? She herself is an amalgamation of generations of powerful women!

As you progress through this book, keep that thought in the back of your mind: behind every incredible character are incredible people. This includes the author of *Geek Girls Don't Cry*, the very book you are currently reading! (That's right, I'm psychic.) When I first met Andrea, I felt an immediate kinship in that we are both women working in male-dominated industries. However, she caught my attention far earlier via social media with her evaluations of my Dungeons & Dragons character, Keyleth. Andrea's introspection and insight into my character's thought process showed how intelligent she is, as well as her observant empathy. What I'm trying to say is, Andrea is a badass, and as I previously stated, those are the only women with whom I consistently associate.

I am deeply honored to not only have a character I created included in this menagerie of matriarchs, but also to write the foreword for this book. As a fellow believer in learning the lessons stories can teach you, I hope you read with an open mind and heart. And let Andrea guide you on how to look at characters critically and from multiple perspectives. Get the most out of storytelling, because the stories that help inform who you are will stick with you for a lifetime.

Happy reading,

Marisha Ray

Marisha Ray is an accomplished voice actor, producer, host, and performer whose credits include video games such as *Persona 3*, *Final Fantasy XV*, and *Star Wars: Battlefront*. She has worked as the Creative Director for *Geek and Sundry*, where she co-created and produced popular shows on gaming, comics, and pop culture. She currently works as the Creative Director for *Critical Role*, the smash entertainment sensation featuring popular voice actors who take on epic *Dungeons & Dragons* adventures.

Marisha lives in Los Angeles with her husband, fellow voice actor and *Critical Role* Dungeon Master Matthew Mercer.

INTRODUCTION

"This isn't a question of what I'm not.
This is a question of who I could be."

—CAPTAIN MARVEL

A
s a woman, I often find myself thinking about what it means when we say a female character is "strong." Does it mean she can kick butt, like Black Widow's introduction in *The Avengers*? Does it mean we can be super, like Buffy Summers and her consistent saving-of-the-world (not to mention consistent tackling-of-homework) in *Buffy the Vampire Slayer*? Or maybe it means women who are deemed "strong" should be celebrated—not because they fight bad guys, but because in the face of issues like post-traumatic stress disorder, anxiety, and depression, they've still managed to show us how powerful and inspirational they are.

Just because some of the most inspirational women in the world are fictional doesn't mean they don't deal with the same issues we face in real life. "There is sufficient evidence to show us those connections we have with these characters, whether it's identification or relatability, are pretty strong,"[i] Andrea Letamendi, a clinical psychologist working at UCLA, told me during an interview. "There's a lot of work that has gone into measuring the strengths of those relationships, better understanding the intensity of those relationships, and even finding a considerable amount of distress when there's a break, when there's a disruption with our relationship in these fictional characters. When we see loss and grieving and disruption in relationships in fiction, it does allow us to be able to process those emotions, to be able to be a little more equipped to handle those emotions. There's a healthy aspect to that."

When I tell people that fictional characters have helped me through some of the hardest periods of my life or have inspired me not to give up on my dreams or goals, I often receive an eye roll or dismissal. It is, unfortunately, a common response—people who aren't familiar with the nuances of pop culture just don't understand why I am able to identify so strongly with a fictional character. But what I wish I could say on more than one occasion is that it's not just about liking an actress that plays the character or feeling like I know that character because I spend my time watching television, playing video games, or reading comics. It's about seeing what she went through— her addictions, her fears, her traumas, her struggles—and applying how she worked through those issues to my own life.

Dana Scully? She helped me become a better student in school, thanks to her choice of profession. Black Widow? She helped me realize I don't have to be defined by the regrets I thought I'd carry around forever. Wonder Woman? She helps me speak up in workspaces and situations where I'm usually the only female in the room, giving me a chance to make my voice heard among the patriarchy. Hermione Granger? She helps me feel confident, allowing me to understand that my "quirky" interests aren't a waste of time and energy but instead are parts of me that are unique and special.

Regardless of what you're going through or what you're feeling, you should never feel devalued because the person who exhibits traits, experiences, or a lifestyle that resonates with you is a fictional character. After all, how is identifying with Katniss Everdeen or Okoye from *Black Panther* different than identifying with a historical figure or author or athlete? More importantly—why are the struggles of *these* characters swept under the rug? Why do we know about the depression Batman experiences after losing his parents but not about Princess Leia Organa's grief after unexpectedly losing her home planet of Alderaan? Why do we know about the alienation Superman experienced after being sent away from his home planet of Krypton but not about Supergirl's trauma, which came from the same experience? Why do we know about Peter Parker's search for purpose after the death of his Uncle Ben but not about Scarlet Witch's struggle with self-esteem in the wake of growing up an orphan?

There has been progress when it comes to embracing women and their accomplishments, but there's still a sharp dichotomy that exists when we talk about female characters as opposed to male characters. That's because it's easy for us to look at men and understand, on the surface, where their issues come from—especially if, like Batman and Superman and Spider-Man, they've been part of our pop culture narrative for decades. But we rarely stop to consider how women deal with concerns like loss and tragedy and depression, because they're so often seen as footnotes in our stories.

Sure, women are seen as "strong" . . . when they're displaying strength in an action-oriented way. That's why we should look beyond a woman's physical prowess and instead focus on the qualities that truly make her strong: her courage in the face of her biggest fear, her will to overcome an obstacle despite being held back by her life experiences, her ability to help others despite her own mental health demons. No matter what we go through in life, and no matter how much our world changes, we *need* these amazing females and their stories to inspire us, to remind us to keep fighting, to help us through our darkest days.

In this book, you'll read about some truly awesome female characters from all areas of pop culture. You'll learn about their lives and accomplishments, but you'll also see how each character's biggest fight wasn't against an alien or a monster; it was against issues like depression, substance abuse, isolation, and anxiety. You'll gain insight from psychologists who have dedicated their professional lives to helping patients find light through mutants, goddesses, and super-heroes. You'll find personal anecdotes and advice from courageous real-life women involved in all facets of pop culture—many of whom credit the characters they work with for helping them through hard times. And, it goes without saying, since these are in-depth analyses of characters and their stories . . . beware of spoilers.

You are important, and your fight matters. You can overcome your fears and your traumas and your anxieties. You can write your own story, no matter who you are or what you struggle with. You can be strong without being a cliché.

But first, you have to believe it.

Part One

OVERCOMING TRAUMA

Research shows that 60 percent of US adult men and 50 percent of US adult women will experience trauma at least once in their lives. Out of those percentages, roughly 8 million people suffer PTSD each year—a statistic the National Center for PTSD claims "is only a small portion of those who have gone through a trauma."[ii]

Given these figures, it's no surprise that we look to people who can help us understand why such trauma took place and how to get through the days when it's hard to smile or show optimism.

At first glance, characters like Black Widow, Dana Scully, Xena the Warrior Princess, Katniss Everdeen, and Storm don't seem like they have much in common aside from sharing the same genre of pop culture. All of these women, however, are survivors. Some, like Black Widow and Xena, were indoctrinated by a life of war and brainwashing. Some, like Katniss Everdeen, Dana Scully, and Storm, found themselves in situations where they were forced to confront their deepest and darkest fears in order to live day by day. But no matter what trauma these women have endured—whether as a Russian spy, an FBI agent, a dystopian teenager, a warlord, or a mutant—the fact that they overcame their brutal pasts and rose up from that 50 percent to empower others and show their strengths is no small feat.

They did it. And we can do it, too.

1

A SPY IN THE RED ROOM

In different ways, trauma attempts to become a dominant fixture in our lives. The lifestyles or moments we experience in our formative years and even afterward stay with us long after we have learned to conquer them, hiding in the shadows of our mind. But undergoing trauma doesn't necessarily mean that we need to be forced into a life where we are defined by what's held us back.

RETCON: In works of fiction, this is a word used to describe a change in a character's history or to describe a different interpretation of previous events important to the character's story.

Like many popular comic book characters, Marvel's® Natasha Romanoff (Black Widow) is a beloved and inspirational hero. Natasha has undergone dozens of **retcons** since her introduction in the 1960s, including her translation to the big screen—the portrayal that she's most commonly known for. But changing her history doesn't change the fact that she's a survivor. And if the world is going to place her on a pedestal, then her personal struggles are important enough to know about.

REPETITION COMPULSION

Natasha was taken from her family when she was just a little girl. She spent her early years in a program known as the **Red Room**, a Soviet facility where young girls were

> **THE RED ROOM:**
> the Komitet Gosudarstvennoi Bezopasnosti (KGB) espionage program where Natasha Romanoff learned the skills that she would later use as Black Widow

trained to become deadly and elite sleeper agents. The Red Room was more than just a training program, however. It used unorthodox methods to make girls like Natasha more capable of spying and killing—methods like brainwashing and biochemical enhancements. Given the type of environment Natasha spent her formative years in, it's no surprise that she entered the world walled-off and emotionless. Before she joined up with the superhero group known as the Avengers, she worked primarily alone, hesitant to get close to or trust anyone, a phenomenon that psychologists call *repetition compulsion*.

"Adults whose childhoods were marred by abuse, abandonment, neglect, or other traumas bring these unhealed traumas along with the defense mechanisms and neuroses . . . into every subsequent intimate adult relationship,"[iii] writes mental health counseling coach Michael Schreiner. While we don't see Natasha pursue any kind of intimate relationship until the movie *Avengers: Age of Ultron*, when she does attempt to romantically engage with a teammate, the subject is not her best friend, Hawkeye, or even Captain America, who's become a close friend and confidant during personal missions. It's Bruce Banner, a man who, when he's not smashing things as his alter ego superhero the Hulk, is nothing more than a mild-mannered and nerdy scientist.

"The flawed unconscious reasoning process behind repetition compulsion is that by setting up similar conditions in adult relationships and finally getting a result of feeling lovable, the pain of the unhealthy primary relationship will be healed, will be retroactively made good,"[iv] continues Schreiner. Natasha gravitates toward the Hulk as opposed to her "safer" teammates because she sees someone similar to herself: a person who is also broken and flawed, traumatized and ostracized by the world. "You think you're the only monster on the team?" Natasha asks Bruce in a quiet moment during *Avengers: Age of Ultron*.[v] The implication of Natasha's question shows what she thinks: that by being with someone who is just as damaged as she is, she can find some closure for the ways in which she was treated and brought up—and she can find love with someone who understands just how much damage she's undergone. Her feelings and choices are a reminder to us that, despite the hero mantle she wears, she still harbors doubts and insecurities pertaining to the life she's worked so hard to leave behind.

THE FEMALE AVENGER

Among the many procedures Natasha underwent as a young girl were "psychotechnics," a process that implanted false memories into her brain; at one point she believed she was a ballerina with Moscow's Bolshoi Theatre, manipulated into escaping to show off her strength. She also endured a serum infusion called the "Kudrin Treatment," a biological treatment that, in addition to increasing strength and stamina, allowed Natasha to stop aging. Perhaps the most traumatic of her experiences with the KGB was Natasha's "graduation ceremony," a sterilization procedure that rendered her infertile. With these treatments, the Red Room made its intention clear: you cannot be a woman who works and have any kind of emotional bond, especially if that emotional bond is with a child.

When Natasha admits to Bruce Banner in *Avengers: Age of Ultron* that because of how she's been raised and what she's done with her life, she can't ever imagine being a mother, she's not just referring to the fact that she's infertile. In fact, I'm sure a well-meaning person in today's day and age would tell Natasha that an inability to conceive is okay and that there are many alternatives she can consider if she wants to have children. But to say that to Natasha would be missing the point she's trying to explain: her experiences have been traumatic, and she's been conditioned to see her profession and motherhood as two completely separate worlds, with no chance of crossover.

While Natasha may be a fictional character, a woman's struggle to feel professionally validated while also embracing motherhood is not a fictional issue. A 2014 *New York Times* column titled "The Motherhood Penalty vs. the Fatherhood Bonus" points out the statistical discrepancy between working men and women and breaks down how having children actually hurts women in the workforce because they're seen as less competent.[vi] And a 2016 Bureau of Labor Statistics report shows that women with young children are less likely to work than men, with only 65 percent of mothers participating in the workforce while nearly 98 percent of men with children had steady employment.[vii] Natasha's feelings speak to the pressure that society has put on women throughout the years and the feeling that they are always perceived as "less"— whether because they can't conceive or because they can and do.

In the same *Avengers* movie, Scarlet Witch casts a spell on the Avengers during battle, giving them visions that are supposed to play with their minds. Natasha's is that of her aforementioned "graduation ceremony." In this vision, we see her forcefully strapped to a gurney, showing she was given no choice before she went under the knife. Although all of her teammates experience visions that haunt them in different ways, Natasha is clearly affected the most, with her memories taking a visible toll on her mind and body; she is unable to complete the fight at hand. Natasha has always been aware of her past and of the events that made her the fighter we watch in different Marvel movies or read about in different comics. But when struck with post-traumatic-like symptoms, she's forced to confront her memories—and forced to ask herself some very real questions. *Am I a good person? Am I really the best person to help other people, since I was brought up so violently? Can people see how damaged I am underneath everything I've built up, even though they call me a hero? After all . . . if I wouldn't even be a good example for my own child, what example am I setting for others?*

WOMEN AND TRAUMA

As previously mentioned, The National Center for PTSD states that 50 percent of US adult women experience trauma.[viii] Women often fly under the radar due to cultural stereotypes, along with the fact that until recently, studies have been designed to cater to males who suffer from trauma.

According to a *VICE* article titled "Women are the Invisible Victims of PTSD," "While the popular perception is that the 'Trauma' in 'Post Traumatic Stress Disorder' has to be something like explosions and war, you can actually get PTSD from any kind of shock and terror. Women are more likely to be the victims of sustained abuse, as opposed to one-time attacks. And they're more likely to experience domestic trauma at the hands of a partner or loved one."[ix] With this in mind, let's come full circle in Natasha's desire to seek out Bruce Banner romantically: in the first *Avengers* film, Natasha has a run-in with Bruce before he's tamed his Hulk persona—when he's not so much a hero as an unchecked manifestation of ruthless anger. Through a series of events, she becomes trapped with the Hulk in his dangerous form and is ultimately forced to defend herself against someone who she stands no real chance of defeating. Keep in mind that, aside from Hawkeye, Natasha is the only member of the Avengers with no superpowers or protective suits to help her. Similar to the aftermath of Scarlet Witch's attack, Natasha comes out of this experience scared and broken.

Natasha is no wallflower; she was trained to kill and proves to be violent, deadly, and calculating. But when faced with impossible odds, she's unable to defend herself. Natasha's experience is particularly jarring because it reminds us that not even a woman as strong and capable as Black Widow can feel empowered or capable in the face of intimate partner violence. Unfortunately, this is an experience that doesn't just exist in a superhero universe; it is a reality that exists for women around the world: The United States Office on Violence Against Women reports that one woman is assaulted every nine seconds, and that domestic violence continues to be the leading cause of injury in the United States.[x]

LEARNING FROM A HERO

Natasha's trauma sits with her for her entire life. She sees her relationships and good deeds as debts to be paid—"red" to wipe out of her ledger[xi]—rather than allowing herself to feel emotions common to those who have experienced healthy friendships and upbringings. In that same respect, she uses defense mechanisms like denial to shield herself from the mindset that convinces her to self-blame for her current situation, even though she was powerless to prevent her trauma.

If Black Widow weren't a fictional character, Natasha might be someone joining a protest in a major city, championing her rights. Hers is a superhero world, however, and much like celebrities, superheroes can't be too open about their personal agendas. Natasha is an Avenger but she's also haunted by the demons from her formative years. By the time Natasha was sent off into the world, she had her own set of issues to deal with, and there was no magical power that she could use to heal herself. She's had to overcome her fears and trauma the same way we do—by finding ways to work through the self-doubt and anxiety that comes with accepting the idea that you don't have to be who you were made to be.

After being saved from the Hulk's attack by her teammate Thor in the first *Avengers* film, Natasha forces herself to continue fighting so that she can save her brainwashed partner, Hawkeye. And at the end of *Avengers: Age of Ultron*, despite her feelings of wanting to run away from a life she doesn't feel she deserves, we see her staying behind to train a new team. In both cases, Natasha overcomes trauma by finding strength in people who believe in her: her best friends and the teammates who have been beside her for years, the ones who unconditionally stand by her even through her worst days. She allows herself to use the skills she has learned in her past when she needs to, but she focuses on using her experiences to help others.

When Natasha was introduced into the world of comics in April 1964's *Tales of Suspense* #52, she was a villain, created to be an antagonist for Iron Man.[xii] That's who Natasha had been taught to be: someone without morals, who didn't care about the lives of others. But when we learn how Natasha fought against her past to make herself stronger and overcome her trauma . . . that's when she becomes our real hero.

A GIRL IN THE FBI

Statistically, there have always been fewer women than men working at the FBI. A 2016 article from *The New York Times* points out that "women hold 12 percent of 220 senior agent positions, including nine who run field offices in places like Los Angeles; Oklahoma City; Louisville, [Kentucky]; and Knoxville, [Tennessee]. That is a decline from 2013, when women held about 20 percent of senior agent jobs and fifteen women ran field offices."[xiii]

In the pilot episode of *The X-Files*, we're introduced to Dana Katherine Scully. We learn that she was recruited out of medical school by the FBI and that she came to the profession of law enforcement with a thesis on Einstein and a degree in physics. By making a decision to become a forensic psychologist and special agent, Scully made a choice that has since inspired and influenced an entire generation of women to work in the fields of STEM—science, technology, engineering, and mathematics. While *The X-Files* is commonly seen as a story about FBI Special Agent Fox Mulder's plight—it was, after all, his sister's abduction years ago that inspired him to open a file on the paranormal—it's Scully who becomes the character viewers identify with when we look for strength and inspiration.

THE "TRAUMA" FILES

Most of the traumas Scully faces in her work are specifically tailored to her as a female, such as her abduction, pregnancy woes, and sexual assault attempts. In this way, her traumas become not just about the cases that she takes on or how she is a woman in a man's world; they become synonymous with living with fear and working through some of the worst days of your life.

When law enforcement officials experience specific traumas such as investigating the scene of a violent crime or witnessing a fatal confrontation, they often experience behavioral and cognitive symptoms. The reactions vary, as a host of personal factors are often at play—how well the agent handles stress, other traumas they may have experienced, and any underlying mental issues or substance abuse issues.[xiv] Although Scully is never diagnosed with a specific mental illness, it's easy for viewers to identify with her struggles of anxiety and depression based on the type of work she deals with. For instance, while she's traveling to various countries and visiting people during cases, she's often exposed to intense violence that weighs on her conscience. Scully also deals with triggers relating to the times she was almost sexually assaulted. At one point, we see Scully abducted out of her own home by a delusional and psychotic conspiracy theorist. In a second season episode titled "Irresistible," she's kidnapped by a serial killer fetishist and nearly murdered. That specific case is one that weighs on Scully even before she's attacked, as she's visibly unsettled by the kind of real-life monster she is investigating. It even causes her to seek counseling from a social worker, bringing up her anxieties about the case. Still, she pushes on, putting work first. Throughout the episode's hour, she claims that she's fine and seems to take it all in stride. But at the end, following her vicious attack, she breaks down in Mulder's arms.

A DAY IN THE LIFE

If you sat Scully down in a therapist's office and asked her if she thinks her life has been traumatic, she would probably laugh at your ignorance. How could her life *not* be traumatic? She's experienced the death of her father, daughter, and sister (and mother, if you count the TV show's revival twenty years later), an abduction, a government conspiracy, countless shootings, sexual assaults, infertility, a rare and barely curable form of cancer . . . and that's just the abridged version. A report from the National Institute of Public Health about PTSD symptoms among law enforcement officials and how those might differ gender-wise notes that significant differences in PTSD symptoms were found in women without a prior history of trauma or military service.[xv] As much as Scully is a trained FBI agent and is certainly capable of handling herself in the field, it's fair to say that her traumatic experiences before being assigned to the X-files were far and few between and certainly were not anything as traumatic as being abducted by a serial killer, shot on multiple occasions, or losing family members because of her work. Scully suffers from a significant amount of survivor's guilt, a psychological condition that occurs when a person experiences extreme guilt because they survived a traumatic event when others did not.[xvi] When Scully gets out of bed every day, she is facing that thought and fear: *Why do I get to keep living and working when the people around me don't? What have I done wrong or right to deserve being given another chance, even though I have found myself in situations even more dangerous?*

Because of Scully's history with personal trauma, there is the possibility that she could have unexpected moments of vulnerability in the field—such as when her dad dies suddenly in the season one episode "Beyond the Sea." Despite her rationale, she believes a death-row murderer who claims he can channel deceased souls, potentially opening a doorway for her to connect with her father. It would probably be more helpful for Scully to talk to her friends, family, or partner about the experiences that weigh on her, but since Scully normally upholds a personality that falls under calm and rational, it's not as easy for her to open up about her feelings.

LEARNING FROM A HERO

Most of us aren't FBI agents in dangerous professions, and the experiences that mess with our heads are more terrestrial than paranormal. But that doesn't change what we can learn from Scully's struggles: the lesson that it's okay to make the decision to get help from someone we trust. If we don't want to see a therapist or a mental health professional, we can trust a close person in our life who has been there for us without judgment: a partner, a spouse, a best friend, or a family member. We can learn healthy coping mechanisms, like diary-writing and exercise, to deal with the anxiety that comes with the traumas we have faced.

In the third season episode "Nisei," an investigation brings Scully into contact with a group called MUFON: the Mutual UFO Network. MUFON is composed of women who are paranormal enthusiasts as well as alien abductees with experiences similar to Scully's. Like many who attend support group meetings of any kind, Scully is initially wary of this group of women, especially since some of them seem to recognize her despite her not recognizing them. But she ends up staying and talking, and in doing so, she starts to recall memories of her own abduction that she'd unknowingly repressed. Scully doesn't bring up all the details because she's not ready to talk about these experiences out loud just yet, which she admits to the group. And they understand, because they've been there themselves; they know what she's been through. This support group helps Scully realize that despite the otherworldly issues she faces, she's not alone.

Most of Scully's traumas aren't visible just by looking at her. Despite the vulnerability she displays, no one would be able to guess how much she's dealing with. Like so many of us who undergo situations such as abuse or traumatic illness, Scully puts on a brave face so she can get through the day and succeed in her work. It's easy to look at her and be awed by her overwhelming strength, but the real show of courage is when Scully admits she needs help.

When Scully was introduced to us in the first episode of *The X-Files*, she represented a different type of female protagonist. This was 1993, and Scully wasn't a blond bombshell. She was short and plain; she wore glasses and a frumpy suit and high heels; she was quiet and soft-spoken. Nevertheless, she walked into Fox Mulder's basement office and didn't back down when he tried to insult her intelligence or her self-worth. She stood her ground because she knew her value; there's a reason why "**The Scully Effect**" exists and why it's a phenomenon named after the woman who defined

THE SCULLY EFFECT: The character inspired numerous young women to pursue careers in science, medicine, and law enforcement and, as a result, increased the visibility of the number of women in those career fields.

what it means to be a "strong" woman in a man's world. (A 2018 study from the Geena Davis Institute on Gender in Media surveyed Scully's influence on girls and women and found that, among other statistics, "nearly two-thirds (63 percent) of women who are familiar with Dana Scully say she increased their belief in the importance of STEM."[xvii])

Because of Scully, we want to believe that we can persevere despite the traumas that try to hinder our successes. And thanks to Scully's perseverance and strength, we know that we can.

AN ICON IN DYSTOPIA

Parental depression can affect children growing up—not just while they're young but well into their lifetime. A 2009 report titled "Depression in Parents, Parenting and Children" notes that "in a given year, an estimated 7.5 million adults with depression have a child under the age of 18 living with them . . . it is estimated that at least 15 million children live in households with parents who have major or severe depression."[xviii] While statistics may indicate this is a large enough number to promote awareness, the *implications* of how depression affects parenting are often ignored.

With the publication of *The Hunger Games* in 2008, Katniss Everdeen—Suzanne Collins's arrow-wielding protagonist from the dystopian world of Panem—entered our cultural landscape and quickly became a character with whom readers could identify. Katniss's personality traits can be summed up in words like *brash, outspoken, callous,* and *prickly*. But it's what she experiences in her childhood and teen years before entering the games that *causes* her to be resentful and distant.

GROWING UP IN PANEM

In the world of Panem, the Hunger Games were designed by the government to be a deadly tournament that forces innocent children to fight to the death against one another. Since no one except the wealthiest of the wealthy is immune to the "**reaping**," Katniss grows up in the shadow of death. By the time Katniss volunteers to take her sister's place in the reaping that will change her (and the world) forever, she already knows there's no other way out of her situation. In fact, it's easy to view her "I volunteer as tribute" moment as a conscious death sentence: the strain of responsibility and the necessity of keeping her family alive pushes Katniss to the brink of depression before she even sets foot in the arena.

> **THE REAPING:**
> a chance lottery for each district of Panem to decide which two citizens will represent the district in the Hunger Games

Katniss grew up in the poorest district of Panem, the impoverished, coal-mining District 12 in the Appalachian Mountains. She was a caretaker from her early days, helping to provide for her family, and this amount of responsibility escalated after her father's death when she was eleven years old. Katniss spent her days caring for a mother with untreated mental illness and a sister too young to take care of herself. Without Katniss, her family wouldn't eat, wouldn't be safe, and certainly wouldn't be able to survive. Katniss has had a damaged psyche for most of her life, and she's unable to vocalize her need for help because so much of her responsibility rests on helping others.

BEING AN ICON

Like other fictional places that the characters in *Geek Girls Don't Cry* encounter, such as Black Widow's Red Room and Ellie's dystopian

America in the video game *The Last of Us*, we don't have a tournament like the Hunger Games. But the situations Katniss experiences are not specific to her fictional arena—we recognize them in the real world in many ways. For example, Katniss's quick indoctrination as a child combatant echoes the struggles of other young people living in military dictatorships. She also experiences combat-related PTSD. Reports show that women are the fastest growing group of veterans, with roughly 27 percent of female Vietnam War veterans struggling with PTSD after returning from combat.[xix]

After Katniss wins the Hunger Games, the Capitol puts her on a pedestal, ignoring her mental health struggles and transforming her into an icon. Her experiences during the games—her near-death moments, the friends she lost, the devastating choices she had to make to ensure her survival—are swept under the rug in favor of crafting her public persona, and all of this builds on Katniss until it overwhelms her. When she becomes the mockingjay, she becomes even *more* isolated as an icon.

As Katniss grows throughout the books—first participating in the Hunger Games, then being forced to participate for a second year in the Hunger Games, and eventually rebelling in all-out war against the Capitol—she loses more and more of her ability to feel safe. This combined with the isolation that comes with being the mockingjay escalates the severity of her already shaky mental health, as she feels like she has fewer and fewer people she can trust and open up to. As evidenced in the second book in the trilogy, *Catching Fire*, when she's thrown back into the Hunger Games after what should be a one-time experience, she comes to the understanding that she can't trust government leaders, who pretend to have her back but are really manipulating her for their own personal gain. And because the government has such an influence on her family (providing them with a home and protection) and her friends (spoiling them with fancy food and clothes), she can't trust the people closest to her for fear that they'll announce how unstable she is to the world or reveal some ulterior motive.

Katniss, like Black Widow, falls into repetition compulsion when she tries to have a relationship with Peeta Mellark, her fellow Hunger Games victor and another trauma survivor. Katniss has known Peeta and her best friend Gale Hawthorn for most of her life, having grown up with them. But it's Peeta with whom she attempts to develop a romantic relationship, because he has undergone the same experiences Katniss has. Similar to how Natasha Romanoff sees Bruce Banner, in Katniss's eyes, Peeta is someone who is also damaged—someone who understands what it's like to be traumatized and used by the government—and who Katniss feels she deserves as a partner.

LEARNING FROM A HERO

Katniss doesn't have outlets that she can use to help herself. She doesn't have a group to talk out her feelings with, and she can't escape the world to take care of herself and her mental health. She doesn't even have the option of a trusted person prescribing her with medication. Even when she's moved to the Victor's Village, an elite and private part of Panem where Hunger Games victors are permitted to live, her new status doesn't make it any easier to find people who can help her. No one is breaking down Katniss's door to give her therapy or medication, so she continues to live in mental anguish as she deals with the fallout from her time in the games as well as the familiar strain of taking care of her family. The best Katniss can do is hope to steal a few moments of peace outside the Capitol's surveillance, where she can participate in activities that remind her of a normal way of life, like shooting with her bow, writing, or taking walks in private—all actions that help her deal with her PTSD.

Whether it's sexual assault, bad family situations, or combat, women work through trauma all the time. They return to society having undergone a psychological experience that's hard to put into words, but through instances like support groups and therapy, they work to put their pain aside so they can continue with their lives and attempt to rebuild what they have lost. They are battling unseen monsters every day in ways that no one ever recognizes—because even if someone else has been there themselves, the pain is always different and the experiences are always unique. Katniss is self-aware enough to know that she'll never be free of her traumas, not even when the Hunger Games cease to exist. The memories will remain and the panic attacks will stay; she will live with her baggage even when she tries to move forward.

Katniss is not, by any definition of the hero archetype, a "perfect" role model. She is simply a girl who had to learn how to fight for her survival against all odds. While most people think the stories of female characters need to have happy, conventional endings that circle back to accepting their struggles, Katniss shows us that's not true. She ends her story with something more important than happiness: hope. Even though she continues to suffer from mental illness and often has episodes that force her to regress into an unstable headspace, Katniss's unconventional ending teaches us that we don't have to be completely healed in order to accept that we have a place in society. Similar to the many women who have come forward in the growing #MeToo movement—women whose traumas have resurfaced thanks to revealing their experiences to the world—we don't have to heal in order to move forward, have a family and a career, and rebuild our lives. We can live with our demons and acknowledge them while recovering. Our life doesn't have to stop because we've experienced something so traumatic that we feel like we'll never move forward again.

Part of the reason Katniss's inspiration and strength is so important is because it comes from the fact that she'll be healing for the rest of her life. She's always going to be damaged, she's always going to suffer from memories she can't escape, and she's never going to be *okay*. Recognizing and embracing that doesn't make us weak. It makes us human.

It makes us victors.

PRACTICING SELF-CARE:
Lessons from Katniss Everdeen

You may not be a victor in the Hunger Games, but self-care comes in many forms. Here are some lessons Katniss can teach us about taking care of ourselves while overcoming trauma:

1. **Make a list of positives.** When Katniss feels overwhelmed, she has a routine to calm herself down: she repeats certain facts over and over again to help her discern what's real and what's not. Focusing on the good things you're lucky to have in your life can help you recognize what you should appreciate and put the negatives into perspective.

2. **Take a walk.** When Katniss goes hunting, it's mostly to help her family survive, but it's also an activity that gives her some peace and quiet. Getting away from your regular environment and into a "comfort zone" is a great way to refocus your mind and help you feel less overwhelmed.

3. **Find a peer support group or a small group of friends with whom you feel comfortable opening up.** Part of the reason Katniss has such a close relationship with Peeta, Haymitch, and other surviving Hunger Games victors is because she connects with people who have similar traumas. Knowing your struggles will be understood by others can help you open up about past experiences.

A WARRIOR IN
ANCIENT GREECE

While the opening theme song of *Xena: Warrior Princess* tells us that "In a time of ancient gods, warlords, and kings, a land in turmoil cried out for a hero," it doesn't specify that this hero, Xena, was thrown onto a path of violence when her village was raided during her teenage years. In a choice that would come to define her, Xena decides not to run from the attack on her village but instead pick up a sword and defend her home, assembling a small group of villagers that includes both her brothers—one of whom is killed in the battle. She is rejected by her mother, who blames her for bringing death to their family and village. Ostracized and forbidden to return home, Xena leans into her warlord nature. She goes on to become known across Ancient Greece as the "Destroyer of Nations": a woman who stands at the head of one of the land's most destructive armies.[xx]

DEFINED BY A PAST

The traumatic upheaval of Xena's experiences in her teens causes her to put up a wall and isolate herself. As a grown woman, Xena gravitates toward and aligns herself with individuals who possess corrupt pasts, because so much of her early life was surrounded by violence.

Xena: Warrior Princess sees Xena attempting to atone for her past sins after being set upon a path of redemption by Hercules. But the transition from ex-warlord to hero is not an easy one. Her unique experience and ostracization lead Xena to feel like she's forced to walk the path of life alone, and since mostly everyone she encounters knows her as a villain, it makes it easier for Xena to retreat into herself when things become difficult both in battle and in her personal relationships.

Throughout the series, for every step forward that Xena takes to right her wrongs, something happens that causes her to take a step back. We see this in many ways, whether through giving in to her violent personality, arguing with her best friend, or choosing not to fight for someone's life. When Xena's mind sabotages her, it makes it hard for her to love and grow and put her past behind her.

SEARCHING FOR PURPOSE

At the beginning of Xena's journey, she's searching for something seemingly simple yet hard to find: purpose. In the pilot episode, after retiring from the warrior lifestyle, Xena literally buries her armor in an attempt to figuratively bury her past. Letting go of the person that has defined her for so long leaves her searching for an identity with which she feels comfortable; she is not a ruthless warrior anymore, but she does not think she deserves to walk the path of good as a savior, either.

Abraham Maslow's hierarchy of needs is a theory of psychology referring to a five-tiered pyramid that shows how people are motivated to achieve certain needs and how some people put certain needs above others.[xxi] According to *Simply Psychology*, "Growth needs do not stem from a lack of something, but rather from a desire to grow as a person. Once these growth needs have been reasonably satisfied, one may be able to reach the highest level, called self-actualization. Every person is capable and has the desire to move up the hierarchy toward a level of self-actualization. Unfortunately, progress is often disrupted by a failure to meet lower-level needs. Life experiences . . . may cause an individual to fluctuate between levels of the hierarchy."[xxii]

Xena experiences much of these "disruptions" on her way to self-actualization. In addition to her mother's rejection, the man she loves dies an untimely death, her friends repeatedly get hurt or killed, and she never gets to tell her own son that she's his mother. But by allowing herself to be seen through the eyes of her best friend, Gabrielle, Xena slowly starts to work through these roadblocks and find a sense of purpose, moving toward self-actualization.

Xena's friendship with Gabrielle begins in an unlikely but fateful way, when the warrior saves her would-be friend's village and then (grudgingly) allows her to tag along on her journey. What Xena finds in Gabrielle is more than friendship—Gabrielle provides the warrior with a safe space, where Xena can be comfortable trying and failing in her journey toward goodness. Once ashamed or closed off to vulnerable feelings, Xena finds that she can open up to Gabrielle easily, which in turn makes her more confident about breaking through the thoughts and memories holding her back from finding self-actualization. Through her best friend, Xena realizes the importance of helping people and working alongside someone you can ultimately trust.

LEARNING FROM A HERO

Just as Scully and Katniss found support systems with their families and with like-minded people who have experienced the same kinds of trauma, Xena finds a support system with someone who understands her and cares for her. It's important to remember that not all of our traumas can be solved by sitting in big groups, and in Xena's case, she learns that having just one person on her side can help her move forward.

Like Xena, you may have a long journey ahead of you. And, like Xena, you may realize that it doesn't matter how strong you are in a battle—your real strength is being able to overcome a past that you thought would forever be a part of you.

A MUTANT IN OUR WORLD

Despite the fact that 11 percent of the US population struggles with claustrophobia and at least 4 percent suffer severely, the phenomenon hasn't been as well studied as other phobias in mental health research.[xxiii] Most people know the character of Ororo Munroe, aka Storm, as a leader of the X-Men, a team of superhero mutant misfits from the Marvel Universe. But many might not know about her fight against claustrophobia and how it affects her everyday life. While Storm's powers include being able to control the weather (which she can manipulate based on her mood) and atmosphere, it is her mental strength that we should be impressed by—the mental strength she's used to overcome a childhood trauma with claustrophobia that nearly resulted in her not taking any kind of "hero" mantle at all.

CHILDHOOD TRAUMA

Unlike some mutants who gain their abilities through otherworldly circumstances, Ororo receives her powers naturally, inheriting them from her mother. However, she doesn't realize she possesses such powerful abilities until after the most traumatic event of her life: when Ororo is a child, a plane shot down by the military crashes into her home, killing both her parents and nearly killing her. Trapped in the ruins of her home with her parents' bodies and reeling from grief, Ororo develops a severe onset of claustrophobia: a fear of small and tight places. "A traumatic event, such as what little Ororo Munroe experiences as a small child, can lead to a variety of symptoms in later life," explains Janina Scarlet, a clinical psychologist who frequently uses pop culture characters in her daily work with clients.[xxiv]

While Ororo spent many years trying to overcome her claustrophobia and anxiety, nothing was a quick fix. Because her emotions were in tune with controlling the weather, her powers often did more harm than good.

PUSHING THROUGH FEAR

Ororo's issues rear their heads repeatedly and in different ways. In *X-Men* #102, during a fight with other mutants that takes place beneath a castle, she loses control of the situation and becomes paralyzed by fear thanks to flashbacks centered on the moments that caused her claustrophobia.[xxv] In *Uncanny X-Men* #147, she responds to her traumatic memories with fury, unleashing the power she's gathered in order to help her teammates escape.[xxvi] Though both responses demonstrate the varying degrees of how people who experience trauma respond to their triggers, Ororo's experiences represent a very real situation for people suffering with this type of mental health issue. "Like many service members who might have endured severe trauma while on deployment, Storm experiences severe panic attacks when she finds herself in a small, enclosed space," explains Dr. Scarlet. "Interventions, such as cognitive processing therapy (CPT), cognitive behavioral therapy (CBT), and acceptance and commitment therapy (ACT) could be beneficial for someone like Ororo to learn to process her traumatic past and to learn to face her fears in an adaptive way."

LEARNING FROM A HERO

On her own, Ororo attempts to manage her claustrophobia by taking her mind off her fears and focusing on coping through actions like meditation; in some of her stories, such as *Wolverine and the X-Men* #24, she frequently tends to a greenhouse that she created at the X-Mansion.[xxvii] This greenhouse, which Storm cultivates in her own time, serves as a personal space where Storm can be alone and take advantage of some much-needed self-care. Since Storm's connection is to the weather, nurturing the lives of the plants and flowers she takes care of is a way to remind her that she's in control.

But we don't always need to go through our struggles alone. Making sure that someone we trust and are close to is aware of what we're dealing with is also helpful, especially when we're in situations where we can't control our own reactions. Not only can these trustworthy friends or family members help us through our issues, they can recognize when we need to step back and take care of ourselves. Although it may be hard for us to admit that we're scared or having trouble, our friends can help us if we let them in on what's going through our head. When Ororo opens up to fellow X-Men team member Jean Grey, it's one of the first times she's able to talk about her past and find that someone else understands what she's feeling.

We can cope with our fears by hiding from them, or we can forge forward with courage even though we are afraid of what we might experience. Ororo is scarred from her past and knows that her fears will always be with her, but she still fights to save the world, becoming a leader.

MARGARET STOHL [xxviii]

@MSTOHL

Margaret Stohl is the #1 *New York Times* bestselling author of *Black Widow: Forever Red* and its sequel, *Black Widow: Red Vengeance*, as well as the *Beautiful Creatures* book series. She was also a writer for two *Captain Marvel* comic series, *The Mighty Captain Marvel* and *The Life of Captain Marvel*. Prior to becoming a published author, she worked in the video game industry, where she still regularly consults on projects.

Q: Who is the female character that you identify with most when it comes to personal struggles, and why?

A: I see elements of myself in both Natasha [Romanoff] and Carol [Danvers, aka Captain Marvel]. Natasha has a brokenness I recognize, where proficiency and exceptionalism are easier for her than intimacy. Carol has the need to save unsaveable people and fix unfixable situations—two of my favorite pastimes. I also identify with [Carol] as only partly human; I too would live on a space station between the world and the universe if I could. Sometimes it feels like I do.

Q: Why do you think we, as artists/individuals, identify so much with characters who have undergone mental health struggles, even though we know they're fictional?

A: I put Carol in therapy in one of the first panels I ever wrote for her, in my issue [number] zero. All heroes have PTSD—women heroes just have that AND the struggle to be respected for how strong they actually are. I think the struggling female hero is a fantasy for me, that I can both be a) strong and b) struggling.

Q: What have the female characters you've worked on in your creative endeavors taught you when it comes to overcoming your own obstacles?

A: We learn from everyone we write. Carol teaches me to lean into my feminism. To not pretend to be anything less than I am. To say the rough thing nobody wants to hear. To lead when I feel like running. Natasha gives me permission to not take shit from anyone, messed up though I may be. It's about role models of strength for me. Strength and power.

Q: What advice can you give to people who might be struggling to find their own light in a dark place?

A: Acknowledge everything—your worst fears, your dark days— to everyone, always. You will be surprised how empowering that can be. Don't give your broken brain power over you. Don't give your demons anything to haunt. Throw open all the windows and let the daylight in.

Part Two

OVERCOMING GRIEF

Grief can be a strange emotion to experience, understand, and conquer. No matter when or to whom it happens, we feel the consequences of it in different ways. While grief itself isn't a disorder, it affects us enough to manifest in a variety of conditions, such as post-traumatic stress disorder and various phobias.

Some of the fictional characters that we view as having the utmost strength have experienced grief: Princess Leia, the face of the Resistance; Mako Mori, the competent Jaeger pilot; Keyleth, the Voice of the Tempest; Captain Marvel, one of Earth's most powerful heroes; and Wonder Woman, the ideal image of resistance and strength. All of these women have experienced losses of varying severity, but they have one quality in common: they don't let their grief stop them from making a difference and moving forward. No matter what their circumstances were, they forged a path for themselves, even where there wasn't one initially.

PRINCESSES DON'T CRY

We are not always prepared when grief strikes. We don't always have a choice about when we need to suddenly flip a switch and become responsible for our emotions. As the leader of the Resistance and arguably one of the most celebrated women in the *Star Wars* universe, you'd never question Princess Leia Organa's strength—largely because whenever we see her, she doesn't show signs of grief or demonstrate emotions that make us believe she's been emotionally compromised. A princess by birth and a steadfast fighter at heart, Leia never seems to falter; she takes on her missions with confidence and determination, proving herself as competent as any male pilot or leader. And when we look at what she's been through in her life, it's easy to see how she earned the title "strongest woman in the galaxy."

MEANING MAKING

Leia's loss comes abruptly and suddenly, when her entire planet is destroyed without warning. When we are first introduced to Leia in

A New Hope, she's being interrogated by Darth Vader, who is seeking the plans for the Death Star and the location of the Rebel base—information that Leia knows but refuses to give up. Already captured and facing possible death, she steadfastly confirms she will not tell the Empire anything, which leads one of Darth Vader's commanding officers to threaten to destroy her entire home planet. Only then does Leia change her mind—and even then, she lies.

She hopes her subterfuge is enough to save her planet and the innocent people who are suddenly in jeopardy, but it's not. Leia watches in horror as her planet is blown up in front of her, and in the blink of an eye, we watch this young princess lose everything: her friends, her home, her family, and her parents, not to mention any valuable or meaningful possessions. A prisoner on a ship coasting through the galaxy, Leia is truly alone and helpless as she watches everything in her life disappear in front of her.

Leia demonstrates a grief component called *meaning making*, a known coping mechanism used by bereaved individuals to make meaning out of their loss.[xxix] When Leia starts fighting for the rights of all the innocent people in the galaxy, she is assigning meaning to the tragedy that she has been dealt while becoming known as one of the leaders of a rebel community, something that will have a lasting impact on the galaxy going forward. "It contributes to the drive she has in leading the rebel alliance," explains clinical child and adolescent psychologist Amy Saborsky.[xxx] "Other evidence that supports this is the bonds she makes with Luke [Skywalker], Han [Solo], and other individuals after Alderaan is gone."

COMPLICATED GRIEF

For people who experience loss and push forward without allowing themselves to think about its consequences, that resilience can lead to the risk of developing something called *complicated grief*: a term that psychologists use to explain how complications can interfere with the healing that comes with prolonged grief. Defined as "a persistent form of intense grief in which maladaptive thoughts and dysfunctional behaviors are present along with continued yearning, longing, and sadness and/or preoccupation with thoughts and memories of the person who died,"[xxxi] complicated grief can become a chronic mental health issue. By refusing to openly address the trauma that she faces, Leia allows herself to remain strong, but she also puts herself at risk for what 10–20 percent of bereaved individuals face every day.[xxxii]

Like those who fight in active combat, Leia does not have time to mourn after experiencing these losses. She does not have time to think about her family, her home, or anyone else who might be affected by Darth Vader's actions. She has to fight and move on or risk being captured and tortured. Leia's struggle mirrors those who experience loss in combat but do not have time to sit and grieve—at least, not until after the fighting has been done. These individuals have to keep going, because it's not an option to be passive about their feelings unless they want to put themselves in danger.

LEARNING FROM A HERO

Leia uses her sense of purpose to move forward. When survivors are able to find meaning in their traumas and tragedies, they can channel their grief into something positive and are also less likely to contact

PTSD. For Leia, this "purpose" is destroying the Empire and saving the universe. She also embraces social support by surrounding herself with people she trusts. After biological families are lost, grief-stricken individuals often look for people they can lean on in order to help them rebuild their lives and relationships, forming chosen families that are not bound by blood but by trust. When the Empire destroys her home, Leia is left with two droids she has befriended (C-3PO and R2-D2) and two men (Han Solo and Luke Skywalker) who have come to her rescue. She trusts them out of necessity, given that she has no else to whom she can turn, but these friends become important to Leia, traveling with her and helping her with her mission against the Empire. Eventually, these individuals become more than just friends—they become a sort of chosen family, and she eventually begins a real one with Han Solo.

Leia's mission, as well as her need to protect the people she cares about, help her cope with her loss because she is able to find meaning in her grief. By surrounding herself with a small but trustworthy social circle and having a focused goal, she can move forward despite losing so much in such a short time.

PILOTS CAN CHANGE
THE WORLD

When we experience grief as a young child, it can impact how we experience the rest of our lives—especially if that grief involves a sudden loss of one or both parents. A report on bereavement during childhood and adolescence estimates "that 5 percent of children in the United States—1.5 million—lose one or both parents by age fifteen."[xxxiii]

Mako Mori, a young Japanese girl, is only ten years old when she becomes an orphan of the Kaiju War. Both of her parents are killed when they travel into town together, leaving Mako to be adopted by Stacker Pentecost, the head of the **Jaeger** Program. You might ask how a girl living with unexplainable grief manages to put everything aside to save the world. But the truth is, she doesn't; as shown at the end of the 2013 movie *Pacific Rim*, when

> **JAEGER:**
> giant robots that can fight monsters. It takes two people to pilot them because of their size. The pilots must be mentally linked to each other in order to stay in sync with the machine.

she saves the world from destruction, she simply learns how to manage her trauma, proving that she can be the hero of her story.

TRAUMATIC GRIEF

Mako experiences traumatic grief when she loses her family—a sudden, abrupt loss. According to Ralph Ryback, PhD, in *Psychology Today*, "it can be extremely painful to experience traumatic grief, as we may find that sentiments and triggers can easily remind us of our loved one. Especially when our loved one's loss was sudden, we may find that thinking and remembering our loved one fuels painful memories and flashbacks that can make us re-experience our loved one's death."[xxxiv] During Mako's first big mission, she experiences an intense bout of PTSD in a flashback that takes her right back to watching her parents die in front of her. Her mental stumble causes her entire mission to be compromised and causes her and her partner to almost die, as she happens to be linked with someone who doesn't know her trauma and for whose safety she is responsible. Like Storm and her claustrophobia, Mako has no choice about when her past will affect her. And like Leia experiencing memories of grief, she has no choice except to address her feelings, because she knows her own life and other people's lives are at stake.

HOLDING ON TO THE PAST

Mako works for the Jaeger Program as a technician, but she desperately wants to become a Jaeger pilot herself in order to avenge her family. Everyone, including her adoptive father, deems her too angry and emotionally scarred to be responsible for the fate of the world. After all, Mako is not only carrying a memory—she is also holding on to her past, which makes it hard for her to move forward. She's consistently haunted by the death of her family in both visible and nonvisible ways; outwardly she dresses in dull blue and gray colors, which are similar to what she wore as a child when her village was attacked, and the blue streaks she wears in her hair (visible throughout the movie) represent the trauma she carries. Inwardly, she's still reeling from the memories of losing her parents. When Mako experiences her PTSD episode, it all but drives home what people around her have been telling her: that she can't be out in the field because she's too emotionally compromised by her grief and memories. "The experience of trauma and grief at the same time can obscure the resolution of our bereavement," Dr. Ryback writes in *Psychology Today*. "As many of us try to hold on to our memories of the person or even [to] tangible objects that are intrinsically valuable to us in fear that we might forget someone who meant so much to us, the normal remembering of the deceased can even end up complicating matters and even causing us more harm."[xxxv]

LEARNING FROM A HERO

Aligning with someone who has experienced the same kind of emotional trauma that we have experienced can be helpful as we try to move forward. Determined to work on her own, Mako didn't think she needed a partner, but she found one in Raleigh Beckett: someone who also experienced grief via the loss of his brother and who is also on a mission to avenge his family. Being with someone who understands her grief is helpful to Mako because it allows her to feel like she has someone who supports her, which in turn helps make her a better pilot. When Mako saves the world, it's not just because of her natural talent or because she's become one of the best pilots around. She saves the world because, thanks to the help of those around her, she's able to turn her grief into something worth fighting for.

DRUIDS HAVE FEELINGS, TOO

Loss is not just relegated to losing parents or friends. Loss can extend to material items, like a home or a sentimental object, or to emotional things, like a goal or an idea that has long been a part of us.

VOX MACHINA:
the name of the first campaign and adventuring group of *Critical Role*, a streaming web show where a group of voice actors play Dungeons & Dragons

Keyleth, a half-elven druid, is a member of the traveling Dungeons & Dragons party called **Vox Machina**. Among a group of gnomes, bards, half-elves, druids, clerics, and barbarians, she possesses powerful and intense magic that comes from both natural ability and a lifetime of training. Despite being the most powerful member of her party, Keyleth is, at her core, a girl with the same insecurities and anxieties that plague anyone growing up, going out on their own, and experiencing emotion like loss and love for the first time. She is a fantasy character in a made-up world, but her emotions and her struggles are entirely human—and it's her determination and strength, not her magical powers, that make her inspirational.

THE LIFE OF A GODDESS

Born with an affinity for spells and magic, Keyleth was raised with a deep love for the elemental and a fierce protection of the lands of her home. But her experience with loss started early in life, and it likely shaped most of Keyleth's childhood and beyond.

Keyleth's mother disappeared when she was young, leaving to embark on her **Aramante** but never returning. This left Keyleth in the care of her conservative father, an archbishop who soon realized the strength of Keyleth's natural abilities. Without warning, Keyleth was torn from a happy, carefree childhood and thrown into a high-stress training program that included massive spell memorization and studying every aspect of ancient tradition.

ARAMANTE: a journey that all would-be druid leaders embark on in order to seek out other tribes, establish relationships, and become a strong leader

This sudden introduction into intense study was a change that likely was extremely traumatic in and of itself, particularly since it was based on the principle that failure was unforgivable. According to the American Psychological Association, children may feel more confident and do better in their studies if they are shown that failure is normal, as opposed to being pressured to succeed all the time.[xxxvi] But Keyleth grows up to see her life's mistakes as more than just simple errors: she sees every mistake as devastating and tied to lasting consequences. When the village of Keyleth's sister tribe is attacked and destroyed by an ancient red dragon named Thorak, Keyleth is quick to blame herself. She descends into grief, assuming full responsibility for what's happened. And after a separate battle that leaves villagers hailing her as a hero, Keyleth experiences a breakdown because she doesn't think she's done anything right—because of her upbringing, she can't think of herself as anyone except a person who brings harm and loss to others.

SMALL TOWN GIRL

Keyleth's childhood mirrors those of children who are brought up in environments where they are over-parented by well-meaning yet overprotective family and then forced into the world without much social interaction. In a *Psychology Today* article, Lisa Firestone, PhD, cautions that "as parents, it is invaluable to be aware of when we are using our children to fulfill our own needs. How much does our desire to protect them come from them? And how much does it come from our own need to act [as] protector? How often are the hugs we give them to provide affection, and how often are they to take affection from them?"[xxxvii] Keyleth's father wanted the best for her, but he also wanted the best for his village and his family history. Although he loved Keyleth more than anything, it's easy to see from the way Keyleth was raised how her father's own needs influenced the way his daughter grew up.

Because of Keyleth's sheltered and focused upbringing, her social skills left something to be desired. Shy and socially inept with hardly any friends from her childhood, she is still more than a little socially awkward when she joins up with Vox Machina. As a result, Keyleth takes a back seat on much of the decision-making, her nervous energy and insecurity about her self-worth causing her to shy away from opening up to a group of people who are trying to get to know her.

ANTICIPATORY GRIEF

From an early age, Keyleth faces pressure from everyone around her in her studies, instilled with a belief that she is supposed to be the leader and savior of her village. By the time she steps out into the wider world to take on her own Aramante, she is not only leaving with the uncertainty of whether she will ever return to her village; she also knows that she is going on the same journey on which her mother lost her life. If that isn't enough, Keyleth is also carrying the weight of her heritage on her shoulders, asking herself while journeying alone if she deserves this life she's been born into.

Because one of Keyleth's biggest fears is the death and loss of those close to her, she closes herself off to any kind of connection or emotion that would otherwise benefit her.[xxxviii] Her fears also keep her from growing relationships with people who want to get to know her and trust her—for example, it keeps her from realizing her love for one of her closest companions: the half-elven rogue, Vax'ildan ("Vax"), who she knows faces impending death based on a deal he's made with a higher being.[xxxix] For a long time, Keyleth is unable to allow herself to love Vax, despite wanting to share her feelings, because of the lingering grief she feels for her future. She knows that, being immortal, there is no choice for her but to watch the person she loves eventually die.

Keyleth experiences what is known as *anticipatory grief*, a practice of mourning that occurs when someone is expecting death. Anticipatory grief often carries the same symptoms people experience after a death has occurred, such as depression, denial, and anger. According to a *Psychology Today* article on bereavement, "to accept a loved one's death while he or she is still alive may leave the mourner feeling as if the dying patient has been abandoned. Furthermore, expecting the loss can make the attachment to the dying person stronger. Although anticipatory grief may help the family, witnessing the grief of family and friends can be very hard for the dying person, who can become withdrawn as a result."[xl]

Anticipatory grief can also extend beyond a living person, as a person can grieve at the anticipation of events like losing a job, the onset of retirement, or a loss of independence due to age or other situations. In addition to Vax's terminal lifespan, Keyleth's grief also stems from the potential loss of something that she's held close to her heart her whole life: her admission that she does not want the burden of her Aramante, something she has been brought up to think of as a part of her.

LEARNING FROM A HERO

Keyleth grew up thinking she didn't need anyone's help to succeed or survive, thanks to her father's strict parenting and his attempts to keep her sheltered. But when Keyleth experiences her breakdown, she finds herself confiding in a former paladin named Kerrek, who allows her to open up about her emotional and mental struggles for the first time. Although it's undoubtedly scary for Keyleth to admit her biggest fears, Kerrek turns out to be the very first person who understands what she's going through, offering her advice about how to look at the big picture and assuring her that things aren't as hopeless as she thinks. It's this conversation that motivates Keyleth to be more confident, showing her that even if we are scared to admit our flaws, having someone to talk to can help us break through some of the darkness.

Similarly, even though Keyleth is hesitant to open up to Vax, he steadfastly stands by her and supports her, encouraging her to pursue her goals. Surrounding ourselves with a supportive "found family" can not only help us move forward but can help us establish lasting relationships that are invaluable. When Keyleth finally tells Vax about her feelings, including the admission that her grief over eventually losing him makes her afraid to love him, it allows her to realize that not everyone will judge you for your fears. Vax's belief in Keyleth helps her believe in herself, reminding her that she has people who care about her even if she thinks she doesn't deserve them.

By the end of Keyleth's journey with Vox Machina, she has evolved from the girl who second-guessed every decision she made and only thought of herself as being a burden to the woman who accepted her anxiety and learned from the lessons it taught her. As Keyleth comes to realize, even if you are afraid of losing yourself to grief, you can always rise from the ashes and be reborn.

PRACTICING SELF-CARE:
Lessons from Keyleth

Keyleth is a master spell-user whose abilities include shapeshifting and ritual casting, and she would be the first to eagerly explain to you how her powers worked. But that's not the only lesson Keyleth can teach us. We can learn a lot about overcoming grief from the half-elven druid.

1. **Start a cycle of encouragement.** One of Keyleth's primary flaws is the fact that she absorbs a lot of guilt, even when she's not at fault. Her Vox Machina companions allow her

to climb out of her self-loathing by helping her focus on her positive accomplishments. Having a network of people who unconditionally support you can be especially important when your emotions are too overwhelming.

2. **Try a form of martial arts or another high-energy activity, like running or boxing.** Keyleth struggles with anger issues, but she takes that anger out by casting new spells and engaging in fights and battles. This type of physical activity is a helpful way to release the negative energy for which she might not otherwise have an outlet. Finding a safe and healthy way to channel your emotions can help clear your mind and help you work through your feelings.

3. **Say an affirmation out loud.** One of Keyleth's famous lines in *Critical Role* is "I bury my shame." This mantra references a time when she killed an innocent creature by accident, and she repeats it for every innocent life she takes, reminding herself that she has to deal with her feelings even if she wants to avoid them. Owning up to her mistake and not hiding it is difficult— but by doing so, Keyleth gives herself permission to embrace her current state of mind. Repeating an affirmation helps you learn how to take responsibility.

HEROES ALWAYS FLY

It's easy for us to look at people who stand in the spotlight—
politicians, historical figures, famous actors—and marvel at how they
seem to have it all together. But we don't know the demons that these
supposed heroes are battling inside their heads. As of this writing, in
the past year alone, our world has been rocked by the suicides of lumi-
naries such as fashion designer Kate Spade and famous chef Anthony
Bourdain. The news of their deaths came as a shock not because of the
way they happened, but because the general public wasn't even aware
these people were dealing with such intense mental health concerns.

A similar case could be made for Carol Dan-

> **KREE**:
> a specific alien-humanoid
> race from the Marvel
> Universe that have at times
> interacted with human
> beings on Earth

vers, a former Air Force pilot who, during a
battle, encounters a **Kree** device and becomes
subjected to otherworldly radiation that gives
her the abilities of flight, super strength, and
energy absorption. Carol became Captain Marvel
by chance, but that didn't make her immune to experiences such as addiction, grief, and self-doubt. Instead,

Carol had to deal with her personal issues while in the spotlight and saving the world on a regular basis.

Like *The X-Files'* Dana Scully, Carol pushed against gender bias to become a fighter pilot, her most well-known profession throughout a long and storied Marvel Comics history. But Carol also took up the mantle of CIA agent and head of security at NASA—professions and fields that are typically dominated by men. It's no question that her independence and determination helped her succeed and thrive, but it's her willpower and strong self-reliance that helped her overcome her demons.

A PERSONAL LOSS

One of the first traumatic losses Carol experiences is the murder of her boyfriend and psychiatrist, Michael Barnett. His death hits Carol hard, not only because he was someone she loved but also because she had been working closely with Dr. Barnett, trying to come to terms with her dual identities of civilian and superhero. Carol—an independent and guarded person by nature—opened up to him about her fears, her issues, and even her powers, and is subsequently forced to feel the grief that comes with losing someone you trust.

When Carol loses this connection, it's the beginning of her isolation. She attempts to start over in California but soon undergoes another round of loss—this time, the loss of her own abilities. This takes place during a fight with another superhero named Rogue.[xli] In an experience similar to those had by people who undergo memory loss from falling into a coma or undergoing an intense injury, Carol loses not only her superhuman powers but also the memories of her friends and family.

Thanks to the help of other mutants, Carol's memories are recovered, but not her emotions. Even though she can still recognize the people she cares about, she has no idea how she's supposed to connect with everyone she used to love—she can't remember her specific feelings toward them. This incident further isolates her, causing her to become withdrawn and confused.

DEALING WITH GRIEF

Mental Health America lists denial, confusion, humiliation, and guilt as some of the emotions that people are expected to feel during grief.[xlii] Carol experiences all of these emotions during her recovery. When the Avengers come to visit her in 1981's *Avengers Annual #10*, they intend to cheer her up.[xliii] Instead, Carol angrily tells them off for abandoning her, pushing them away in her time of need. Although Carol knows that she should accept help, she's too angry and raw from her experiences to understand that people are offering help.

As Carol moves through life gaining new powers and reforging important relationships, she continues to carry her grief with her. Not surprisingly, everything she's experienced eventually catches up with her and takes a toll on her mind. Like Princess Leia Organa, Carol experiences complicated grief—but in Carol's case, the "person" who she is grieving over is her teammates, her powers, her friends, her family, her memories, and the hero lifestyle to which she has adapted.

UNHEALTHY COPING MECHANISMS

Grieving doesn't take a backseat for anyone, and it certainly doesn't for Carol, someone who has duties to uphold and people to protect.

Like Storm, she forges ahead despite her demons rearing their ugly heads, because she knows that she has a job to do. Because of Carol's independent attitude, however, she doesn't talk to anyone about her emotional distress, and her complicated grief leads her to fall on alcohol as a coping mechanism.

"Some individuals may engage in maladaptive coping behaviors such as withdrawing from others and/or substance abuse," says Dr. Scarlet. "These coping behaviors may reduce the individual's struggling in the short term but may actually increase that person's emotional suffering in the long term." Carol hides her alcohol dependence from her teammates instead of opening up to them and goes on Avengers missions while intoxicated, making dangerous errors that cause her friends to become concerned about her.[xliv]

"Unhealthy coping mechanisms is the last thing she may want to do to recover," adds Dr. Saborsky. "When someone suffers a trauma like Carol, it is more beneficial for them to work on tools that will help them move forward, remember the situations that they are suppressing, and face emotions that were traumatic for them." For Carol, this tool manifests in her teammate, Tony Stark, otherwise known as Iron Man. Having had problems with the same kind of addiction, Tony is able to provide context for the emotions that Carol is dealing with, allowing Carol to feel comfortable opening up. More importantly, Carol starts to see that she can take responsibility for her actions, knowing that someone is there to help her heal.

LEARNING FROM A HERO

It's easy to get mentally stuck and keep everything locked up inside when we've had traumatic experiences. Often, we want nothing more than to take to the sky in the way Carol does—soaring away from our troubles, to the stars and beyond. But finding friends you can trust and who care about your well-being can make a difference. When Carol was at her lowest, it was the Avengers who helped her through her addictions and her feelings. And even though she pushed them away, they were still there for her when she needed someone with whom to talk, which helped her move forward and even strengthened her friendships with them.

Like Leia, Carol also took advantage of establishing a found family. While Carol was recovering with the X-Men after her accident, she found that bonding with another team helped her feel like she belonged somewhere. Like Xena the Warrior Princess, although Carol thought she lost the parts of herself that she felt defined her, she found a purpose with the X-Men. Carol realized that even though she didn't have her powers, she still had her intellect and sharp skills—abilities that made her an asset in a fight even without super strength.

One of Carol's most notable mentors, Helen Cobb, makes her debut in *Captain Marvel* #1, the 2012 series helmed by writer Kelly Sue DeConnick.[xlv] Helen is a fellow pilot who reminds Carol to be the best she can be and to not let anything hold her back. It's a simple lesson, but an important one. Although it's a lifelong journey for Carol to overcome her inner demons, we can find inspiration from her. We can all punch our own holes in the sky.

AMAZONS ARE WARRIORS

The visibility of female role models, especially in the world of pop culture, has always been important. But we generally don't think of these female role models in terms of their mental strength. We think of them in terms of what they represent outwardly: pride, determination, and physical strength.

There's a reason so many of us wanted to be Wonder Woman when we were younger and why, when she finally appeared in her own film, she immediately began to inspire an entirely new generation. Even before she became a superhero whose name was instantly recognizable as part of our pop culture lexicon, she stood for everything we were looking for in a role model: acceptance, compassion, justice, and courage.

But those came from more than just her physical strength.

EMPATHETIC COMPASSION

Created by psychologist William Moulton Marston as a way to "smash the patriarchy" in a world filled with male heroes, Wonder Woman debuted in 1941 as the world's first female superhero.[xlvi] Throughout her long history in pop culture, Diana of Themyscira (also known as Diana Prince) has taught us how to find strength and fight for justice. While Diana is a world-class fighter who uses her magical lasso of truth to aid her in battle, her most important asset is not her fist or a weapon—it's her compassion.

In both the comics and the 2017 *Wonder Woman* film, Diana routinely experiences moments of compassion that are radically different from what we've seen in other superheroes. What Diana exhibits—a term psychologists call *empathetic compassion*—is not a bad quality. In fact, it's refreshing to see a superhero who is so aware of other people's emotions. But "too much empathy can be debilitating," cautions Tara Well, PhD, in a *Psychology Today* article. "When we become too distressed about the suffering of others, we don't have the cognitive and emotional resources available to do much to help them. Having compassion, a cognitive understanding [of] how they're feeling, is better for our own well-being and the well-being of those in need."[xlvii]

Because Diana was raised with feelings of responsibility and trained with a duty to protect the world, this empathetic compassion actually causes her emotional grief. She wants to help everyone and save everyone, but when she can't, she becomes stressed and upset about what she can't control and who she can't save. She feels responsible for trying to make the world a better place for *every* individual, and she feels pressure that she's failed when she can't save everyone.

A GODDESS AND HER LOSS

Diana's grief comes from losing both herself and those she loves. In the *Wonder Woman* film and comic books, Diana tragically loses her friend and love interest, General Steve Trevor, when he sacrifices himself to save the world. Diana already knows she will outlive anyone she gets close to since she's immortal, but then she has to suddenly grapple with the unexpected death of someone with whom she has fallen in love. To Diana, an innocent life was taken, and she was at the root of the cause. Similarly, in the 2005–2006 comic event *Infinite Crisis,* Diana (as her civilian self and not Wonder Woman) is caught on a worldwide broadcast killing a civilian as a last resort to save the world. Haunted by the trauma of taking an innocent life, Diana puts herself in a self-imposed exile for one year, hiding from society, ashamed of what she has done.

It's not uncommon for those of us experiencing grief to close ourselves off, both mentally and physically. "People who, like Wonder Woman, face frequent combat may occasionally engage in a behavior that goes against their morals. This is called *moral injury,*" explains Dr. Scarlet. "When an individual experiences moral injury, they may feel guilty and ashamed of themselves or their actions. However, by reconnecting with one's core values, such as by continuing to help others, by connecting with loved ones, and by discussing and processing the painful event, people can return to their superhero selves just as Wonder Woman does."

When Diana returns from exile and decides to rejoin the world, she starts working again under her civilian alias, helping people who are in trouble. She realizes how much of humanity she has missed out on by closing herself off, and the act of helping people—along with rediscovering her compassion—helps her heal and move on.

LEARNING FROM A HERO

In the *Wonder Woman* film, when Diana comes to London with Steve after leaving her Amazon home, she is quick to notice how different humans are and how flawed the greater world is. She teams up with

Steve and a few other World War II fighters, and her subsequent travels and battles not only allow her to witness war, they allow her to witness the people it affects. In the final showdown of the film, she reminds Ares, the god of war, that compassion is her greatest strength—allowing herself to recognize that while her empathy may be one of her flaws, it's a flaw she can embrace and use to make herself stronger.

Diana chooses not to channel her anger into revenge or rage, but rather to dedicate her newfound knowledge of human life to making the world a better place. It would have been easy for Diana to turn to violence in her grief, but thanks to her compassion, she is able to use her powers for good. She recognizes Steve's death as a way of preventing more suffering, which allows her to put her grief into perspective.

As much as we want to be responsible for changing the world by smashing the patriarchy with our fists, smashing the patriarchy with our personality can make a greater difference. As Diana shows us, qualities like compassion and empathy are significantly more powerful than physical strength—and just as important when it comes to being a superhero.

HOW TO BE: Geek Girl Strong

What is one of the best ways to get through a tough time, clear your mind, and release your emotions?

Being active. But don't take Katniss Everdeen's, Black Widow's, or Jessica Jones's words for it. According to a journal study from the National Institute of Health, "Many studies have examined the efficacy of exercise to reduce symptoms of depression, and the overwhelming majority of these studies have described a positive benefit associated with exercise involvement."[xlix]

There's no doubt about it: taking the time to work out, even with a small effort, can go a long way toward improving your mental health. And if you're going to be active, why not be active like the superhero you really are?

From feminist and geek Robyn Warren, [EdM], founder of the health-coaching community *Geek Girl Strong* (www.geekgirlstrong. com), here are two workouts that we promise will make you feel like a superhero—without even leaving your house.

LARA CROFT WORKOUT

1 Minute of Crab Walks	20 Jumping Jacks
50 Jumping Jacks	10 Dead Bugs
10 Skater Lunges	10 Jumping Jacks
40 Jumping Jacks	10 Back Extensions
10 Push-ups	5 Jumping Jacks
30 Jumping Jacks	5 Burpees
10 Squats	

MISTY KNIGHT WORKOUT

7 Rounds of:

3 Walkouts	10 Tricep Dips
5 Push-ups	15 High-to-low Planks

KELLY SUE DECONNICK[xlviii]

@KELLYSUE

Kelly Sue DeConnick is a comic book and television writer who has worked for Image Comics, BOOM! Studios®, Oni Press, comic book publisher Humanoids, Dark Horse Comics®, DC Comics®, DC Vertigo®, and Marvel Comics. She is best known for her run on Marvel's *Captain Marvel* and Image's *Pretty Deadly* (which she cocreated with Emma Ríos) and *Bitch Planet* (which she cocreated with Valentine De Landro).

Q: Who is the female character that you identify with most when it comes to personal struggles, and why?

A: I don't really identify as having mental health issues—though I know that's rubbish. I have a history of addiction issues, which is a diagnosable mental health issue, and I struggle with stress same as pretty much everyone else living in 2018. But it's not a thing I really spend much time thinking about, and it's certainly not a prominent part of my identity. I feel bad saying that, as I'm afraid it sounds like "yes, but not ME," but at the same time, I think if you're pretty neuro-normative, it's BS to pretend you're not.

Q: **Why do you think we, as artists/individuals, identify so much with characters who have undergone mental health struggles, even though we know they're fictional?**

A: Why do we identify with any character even though we know they're fictional? Because that's the purpose of story. Why does your mouth water when you imagine biting into a lemon? Because it's through story that we practice life.

Q: **What have the female characters you've worked on in your creative endeavors taught you when it comes to overcoming your own obstacles?**

A: You know who was important to me? Maggie Estep. Maggie was a real woman, an artist, an addict, and a junkie and my AA [Alcoholics Anonymous] and NA [Narcotics Anonymous] sponsor. Maggie was wildly imperfect, but I loved her and she loved me and she believed in me when I was a train wreck. Maggie's been dead for a couple years now, but she still gets me through.

Q: **What advice can you give to people who might be struggling to find their own light in a dark place?**

A: I would not presume to advise those whose struggles are not my own. To the addicts who may be reading this, I would say, "You think you're special and you're not." And there's great freedom in that. Find your community of sober drunks and clean junkies and there you will find unconditional love and a way to live and work.

Part Three

OVERCOMING
ADVERSITY

Adversity, defined by Meriam-Webster as "a state or instance of serious or continued difficulty or misfortune,"[i] can affect one's life in different ways. As women, we are prone to coming up against adversity that is specific to our gender, such as workplace bias or judgments about appearance. But there's a reason why a study published by the Proceedings of the National Academy of Sciences (PNAS) concludes that, after researching 250 years of history, women on average have lower mortality rates compared to men.[ii] It's because we are resilient in the face of setback. We live longer, work harder, and push forward more steadily.

Still, this observation from the World Health Organization is worth noting: "Gender determines the differential power and control men and women have over the socio-economic determinants of their mental health and lives, their social position, status and treatment in society and their susceptibility and exposure to specific mental health risks."[iii] As the women in the following chapters demonstrate, it's a long and sometimes tough road to overcome adversity. And because the definition of the term is so all-encompassing, anyone can be thwarted by obstacles, no matter how significant. If something impairs your mental health and prevents you from moving forward, it is considered an adversity—something we must learn to conquer.

For Penny Rolle, it was overcoming expectations of the patriarchy. For Barbara Gordon, it was overcoming a physical tragedy. For Jemma Simmons, it was overcoming otherworldly and unfamiliar situations. For Jennifer Walters, it was overcoming trauma. And for Hermione Granger, it was overcoming her own intellectual gifts.

I AM PROUD OF WHO I
HAVE ALWAYS BEEN

As women, we face discrimination and judgment throughout our lives, and it doesn't go unnoticed. According to the World Health Organization, "gender-specific risk factors for common mental disorders that disproportionately affect women include gender-based violence, socioeconomic disadvantage, low income and income inequality, low or subordinate social status and rank, and unremitting responsibility for the care of others."[liii]

When writer Kelly Sue DeConnick and artist Valentine De Landro introduced the world to the character of Penelope "Penny" Rolle in the 2015 comic book series *Bitch Planet*, their goal was simple: show the world that strong, feminist women exist and that they don't have to fit a stereotype of what we expect women to be and look like. But Penny, with her plus-sized body and mixed race and loud confidence, became so much more than a character in a comic book. She became an ideal, a representation for women everywhere—one that said even if you didn't look like Penny, you had something that was different than what society

> **BITCH PLANET:**
> a place where women are sent if they are deemed "noncompliant." There they live in jail and are forced to participate in battle royales with one another.

"expected" of you, whether it was hair color, skin color, or political belief. And if you *did* look like Penny, you finally had someone you could relate to both emotionally and personally.

The moment Penny is forcibly removed from her home and taken to **Bitch Planet**, she begins a struggle to overcome those who tell her that her appearance and personality will never be acceptable. But from the very beginning, Penny is "noncompliant" and proud of it. She never fails to fight back. And even though she fights harder than most of the other women in this book, we identify with her not because of her raging temper but because of her determination, confidence, and belief in herself.

DEFINED BY A CULTURE

Penny had a stable and loving life growing up, and although she never fit into the mainstream norm, she never wanted to. She learns how to survive on her own from an early age, eager to be independent even though she knows she can ask for support; in a flashback to Penny's early life, we see her cooking with her grandmother and refusing even the simplest offer of help. Despite her preference for independence, we see her grandmother as a source of happiness and encouragement—someone who allows Penny to be herself, despite how society sees her.

Bitch Planet uses the idea that you don't have to have a "problem" to be someone who is shuttled off to a prison that tries to keep you away from society. Instead you can be "revoked" and removed for simply existing. For Penny, her "problem" is that society sees her skin color and weight as qualities not in line with the social norm. Because of that, she is constantly pushed up against walls, struggling to make her voice heard among louder and more "socially acceptable" individuals.

A different flashback shows Penny called to the office at school for getting into a fight with a boy. When Penny is coerced into trying to admit there was no reason for her to fight, she stands up for herself and defends her actions. As Penny tries to steer the conversation, she is shut down and pushed away, a very real representation of how women are treated if they do not "behave" in society.

EMBRACING INSECURITIES

In issue #3 of *Bitch Planet*, Penny is placed in a room with computer screens that she's told will render a version of her "ideal" self. Initially afraid of what she'll see, Penny realizes that her ideal self looks exactly like her—hair color, size, and all. When the technicians assume something is wrong based on the fact that Penny *likes* her appearance, Penny simply laughs because she knows that she is confident about how she looks, and no one can take that confidence away from her or break her.

Sometimes the hardest lesson for us to learn is how to accept the fact that we're happy with ourselves. While insecurities (especially those about physical looks and inner feelings) will always be a roadblock, "recognizing [when] you've been manipulated into feeling this way can help you shake aside that negative self-assessment," says Susan Krauss Whitbourne, PhD, of *Psychology Today*.[liv] What the people in *Bitch Planet* were hoping to see was a stereotypical woman who is unhappy with her looks, but that's not what Penny shows them. She shows them her ideal version of herself: the person she's always been. She recognizes that she's happy with how she looks and feels and that she doesn't need to change herself to fit in like everyone assumes.

LEARNING FROM A HERO

If Penny can teach us anything, it's that learning to love yourself is the greatest motivator for overcoming adversity. Penny doesn't let other people influence her impression of how she should be seen. She doesn't let the opinions of others change what she's proud of when it comes to her looks or personality. Finding that confidence by surrounding yourself with family or close friends who unconditionally support you—like Penny's grandmother—can help you increase your confidence and positive outlook.

Though not everyone has blood family they feel comfortable opening up to, a found family is just as important. The inmates that Penny befriends at Bitch Planet all support her when she stands up for herself and continue to have her back when she goes up against the men who are trying to force her into being compliant.

The comic landscape of *Bitch Planet* lives in a dystopian world, but the issues that Penny deals with are far from fictional or dystopian. Penny shows us that the simple act of loving ourselves can help us overcome any obstacle without compromising on what makes us unique.

12

I AM PROUD OF
WHO I BECAME

For those who protect us—on the streets, in the field, or overseas—keeping the world and our loved ones safe comes with a price. That price? The repercussion of dangers that threaten their profession . . . and their lives.

Barbara Gordon, daughter of Gotham Police Commissioner Jim Gordon, has a PhD in library science and works in Gotham city's public library—by day. By night, she has a different job entirely, using her smarts and skills to stop crime while bringing justice to innocent people. Although Barbara Gordon is commonly known to comic aficionados as Batgirl, she isn't the first—and won't be the last—to wear that particular superhero mantle. Yet she is the one most readers remember and the one we tend to connect with most, not because of her fighting skills but because of her resilience in the face of overcoming a very specific adversity.

THE KILLING JOKE

In the well-known 1988 comic arc *The Killing Joke*, Barbara Gordon is shot in her apartment by supervillain the Joker, an injury that leaves her paraplegic and unable to complete her duties as Batgirl. Suddenly confined to a wheelchair, Barbara is forced to not only give up the crime-fighting part of her life but also the simple things she's taken for granted, such as walking, dancing, running, and even moving easily across a room. Barbara now feels weak and misunderstood, and she fears losing her mantle as a hero because she's no longer able to physically help people. Barbara's resulting PTSD and depression mirror symptoms similar to what many service members and first responders with similar injuries experience: intrusive memories, hypervigilance, and mood changes.[lv]

Barbara is a human—as a vigilante, she does not have powers of any kind, and she relies on her physicality and mental acumen rather than a magical lasso of truth or super strength. But perhaps the most human quality about her is that she struggles deeply with mental health issues while adjusting to her paralysis. Not only is Barbara physically scarred from her trauma, she is emotionally scarred as she deals with how to navigate a new disability, dealing with traumatic nightmares and memories that signal a level of guilt and helplessness. In *Batgirl* #16,[lvi] Barbara pays her psychologist a visit and talks openly about her dreams of wanting to kill the Joker. Barbara admits that when she wakes up and realizes it's not a dream, she sometimes feels sad but also feels angry. Barbara recognizes that her life has changed, and she has to deal with the mindset and thoughts that come with experiencing a traumatic and near-fatal event.

WOMEN AND DISABILITIES

According to statistics, "about 10 percent of the world's population, or roughly 650 million people, live with a disability."[lvii] For women, living with a disability—physical or mental—often means they face added obstacles in addition to the ones that come with every-day life. Women experience marginalization in work and at home and face greater barriers when it comes to getting help and support, with USAID noting that women and girls experience "disproportionately high rates of gender-based violence, sexual abuse, neglect, maltreatment and exploitation."[lviii] And for those like Barbara, who have been injured on the job or whose daily lives revolve around a livelihood that has been disrupted because of a setback, it's not uncommon to have feelings of depression or anxiety following the traumatic event.

"People like Barbara Gordon, who are injured and need to take time off from work or retire due to a disability, may believe themselves to be 'weak' and 'broken,'" says Dr. Scarlet. "As a result, some individuals may struggle in finding ways to connect with what's most meaningful to them, such as helping others." This struggle is Barbara's main source of frustration. As a vigilante, her life's purpose as someone who helps keep the world safe has become synonymous with being out on the streets and physically protecting people. When she's paralyzed, she feels like her disability has taken something important away from her and that she can no longer be useful. But working through her self-doubt and depression, she eventually realizes that while she can't walk properly or run along rooftops anymore, she can still be helpful by using one of her greatest assets that *hasn't* been taken from her: her mind. When Barbara starts to embrace her new life as the superhero known as Oracle, helping Batman and other vigilantes in Gotham fight crime from behind a computer, she succeeds by using her brilliant brain, her exceptional memory, her knowledge of science, and her familiarity with the law enforcement world. These are traits that Barbara has always possessed, but when it came to facing off against bad guys, they usually took a backseat to punching and fighting. Having these qualities manifest themselves so strongly after her injury helps her realize that she can still be important, strong, and knowledgeable, even if she can't be mobile.

LEARNING FROM A HERO

It's easy to feel isolated when something happens that sets us apart, but by hiding this part of ourselves, we're only hurting ourselves more.

Barbara shows us that there's no shame in seeking help and that even the strongest and most independent superheroes need a support system. These people don't need to be therapists; just seeking out someone who can offer an outside opinion can be helpful. As Dr. Scarlet explains, "therapy and other modes of support can help individuals like Barbara Gordon find their other superhero abilities and help them become a new version of a superhero." Some organizations encourage trauma survivors to speak openly about their experiences. Joining a support group and talking about how common mental health issues are not only helps spread the awareness of PTSD, but it also helps others to feel less alone.

Like Princess Leia finding purpose after experiencing grief, Barbara finds strength and meaning in her journey towards healing and in the new identity she's created for herself. Being behind a computer is not the same as being on the street, but by accepting her injury and realizing how she can still be useful to the world, Barbara finds a way to overcome one of her biggest setbacks. Barbara works through her self-doubt and depression to embrace her new life, proving that sometimes you don't need to physically disarm a criminal in order to help save the world.

Session Notes:

"There's no cure. There's no 'you're free of all your anxiety until the end of time,' but [there is] more of a realistic approach to 'you will gain insight, you will gain an ability to reflect, you will gain emotional intelligence, you will overcome those fears and self-doubts.' But you will never be absolutely free of those insecurities and especially of those clinical systems [Barbara Gordon] was experiencing with those flashbacks and nightmares relating to the Joker. I think this is a story that is unique to comics and probably one of the most important stories that needs to be told. Because it tells us she still has her trauma, but she is not her trauma. That doesn't define her. But she has to get out of that headspace and she has to do a lot of reflective and therapeutic work with a person, a therapist, to understand."

—Andrea Letamendi, PhD

13

I AM PROUD OF
WHO I WANT TO BE

Where we grow up and spend our time is where we become comfortable. We adapt to our environment. If we are suddenly pulled out of a comfortable setting, we may find ourselves not only having to overcome a changed mental state but also having to overcome obstacles that accompany being displaced.

Despite repeatedly overcoming roadblocks to learn new scientific formulas and push the boundaries of what her professors could teach her, *Agents of S.H.I.E.L.D.* character Jemma Simmons never thought that she would come face-to-face with challenges that would threaten her life, the lives of her friends, and the world. To succeed and survive trials like being marooned on an alien planet for months with no human contact and being trapped in a bunker underwater, Jemma had to not only rely on her scientific and logical thinking to overcome the challenges that stood in front of her—she had to step up and learn how her own strengths could be assets even in unfamiliar situations.

THROWN INTO THE WILD

If you were to call Dr. Jemma Simmons smart, you would probably be underselling the fact that at seventeen years old, the biochemistry genius already had two PhDs to her name. A longtime lover of science and learning, Jemma was never content to stay in one place for too long. She was always looking for the next big opportunity, whether it was through work, her academic studies, or personal and professional relationships. However, as much as she wanted change, the environments she chose were, more or less, familiar—friends and professors she knew, places she was used to traveling, and work in which she was trained. Recruited into the new S.H.I.E.L.D. (Strategic Homeland Intervention, Enforcement, and Logistics Division) team by Special Agent Phil Coulson, Jemma was hired with the intent of running the science team—designing specialized equipment to be used in emergency situations.

Jemma was displaced from a familiar environment when she joined the team at S.H.I.E.L.D. Although she was with her best friend and doing work she was familiar with, the environment was a striking change. It's not surprising that Jemma was at risk for trauma even before she started experiencing challenging events; according to a study on the effect of displacement and mental health, "better understanding short- and long-term effects of displacement could provide better early intervention as related to long-term effects of anxiety, depression, and PTSD."[lix]

One of Jemma's first missions involves her traveling to Peru to investigate a special object of unknown origin, where she's captured by Peruvian rebels. Managing to escape, she then has to face an armed takeover of S.H.I.E.L.D.'s ship. On another mission, Jemma is infected with an alien virus, causing her to be quarantined in her lab. She tries to use all her science knowledge to find a cure, but when she can't, she attempts to save the team from becoming infected by jumping out of the plane. Jemma's defining qualities have always been resourcefulness and stubbornness, but without control over a situation, Jemma is thrown headfirst into challenges that she's not used to dealing with—making it hard to overcome them, especially if she can't use familiar scientific methods.

ALIEN PLANET, POPULATION: One

For 4,722 hours (roughly six months) Jemma is marooned on a desolate, unforgiving planet called **Maveth**. It lies so far away from the sun that there is never any natural light. Constantly threatened by a terrifying predator, struggling to survive on her own, and unable to contact any family or friends, Jemma has no way to know if she'll ever be rescued. She doesn't know if she'll ever see her home or have the simple comforts of food and water again.

MAVETH:
After S.H.I.E.L.D. took control of an alien artifact, it was supposed to remain locked away, only to be used for testing purposes. But when it was accidentally "awakened" in Jemma's presence, it took control of her, transporting her through a portal to this alien planet. *Maveth* is Hebrew for "death."

Studies have shown that while mental health disorders vary in correlation with forced internal displacement, the most notable ones that do occur are PTSD, anxiety, and depression. Jemma's desperation reaches several breaking points, when she comes close to giving up despite trying to stay hopeful and use her science-inclined mind to find a solution. By the time she is finally rescued and brought back to Earth, she is shaken and traumatized by her experience. But just because her experience has ended doesn't mean her trauma and pain fade. She's haunted by nightmares of the monster that lurked in the shadows, and she's terrified of being alone.

"That sense of social isolation and also additional, complicated trauma leads to distancing, further isolation, and difficulty processing closeness," explains Dr. Letamendi. "Even just, 'how can I resume the life I used to have when I've seen things that I can't unsee?' These are complex traumas." Jemma's depression and loneliness manifest in the form of PTSD in the same way that it does for individuals whose populations are affected by displacement and combat. Jemma is someone who has always had all the answers and who is used to fixing any problem that comes along, no matter how unique. But she can't figure out how to fix herself—and that is a struggle that is hard for her to accept.

Jemma is a scientist before anything else. She is someone who looks for the patterns and weak links and figures out a solution within the variables she can control and understand. But as she comes to realize, there is no cut-and-dry solution for overcoming the kind of displacement she has experienced.

LEARNING FROM A HERO

After we experience a traumatic event, our first instinct is to hide our feelings, whether out of complex shame and guilt or because we think no one else will understand what we've been through. This is especially true for Jemma, who refuses to talk to anyone about her nightmares or her PTSD. Eventually, Agent Coulson allows her to open up by reminding her that he, too, has experienced something that no one else understands; he was brought back from the dead by alien technology after being killed by the Norse god Loki.

"When addressing her changes in worldview, her changes in herself . . . just holding on to the thought that you're alone in your traumatic experience can lead to feeling like 'I'm on Mars, I might as well just be by myself,'" says Dr. Letamendi. "That sense of separation and distancing is very common with people who have very unique and complex traumas. And they feel forever changed." Knowing that she has someone in her corner who won't judge her and can relate to what she's going through—someone else with a scar that can never fully heal, both literally and figuratively—helps Jemma feel more comfortable about accepting her own trauma. Being around someone who is real and truthful about their own struggles can help us to work past our mental roadblocks, and Jemma shows us that we don't have to be trained in battle to be strong—we can use strength of mind to help us through our darkest days.

I AM PROUD OF
WHO I WILL BE

We all deal with monsters that live in our past, and we also each have sides that we're sometimes scared to show the world. Being human means having emotions, but sometimes these emotions can become more than just a part of you—they can become a hindrance.

Jennifer "Jen" Walters can be considered one of the most accomplished women in the Marvel Universe®. As an attorney, she spends her days as a civilian superhero, fighting for innocent people's rights and using her determination, smarts, and mental strength to make the world a better place. And as She-Hulk, she spends her days running around the city as a superhero of another kind, protecting the world from otherworldly evil. Unlike her cousin Bruce Banner, who received his powers from a science experiment gone wrong, Jen's power came from a blood transfusion from Bruce that she received when seriously wounded. Possessing super strength, endurance, and a quick healing ability, Jen has always been able to control her hulk persona, retaining her intelligence and personality even when she's not her human self.

But Jen's biggest adversary has always been her own emotions. Like anyone keeping a volatile being inside them, Jen struggles with fear and panic while also dealing with all the feelings and challenges that come from being human—and from the added pressure of being a working woman in a high-profile profession usually dominated by men.

TWO PERSONALITIES

Jen understands that her hulk persona is a characteristic of her personality and struggles with trying to balance it with the human part of herself. Famed psychiatrist Carl Jung wrote about his own two personalities in his autobiography. As licensed clinical and forensic psychologist Stephen A. Diamond wrote in a review of Jung's work, "to have a persona is not the problem. We all need a persona, as we all need an ego. But the trouble begins when we become overidentified with the persona or ego, believing that these artificial creations totally define our identity."[lx] For some time, Jen felt more comfortable in her She-Hulk form than her human form, thinking that she was more confident and assertive. But she gradually realized that it didn't matter whether she was "hulking" or human—she had something to offer the world in both forms. As She-Hulk, she could use her physical strength and confidence to fight with the Avengers. As the human Jen, she could use her emotional strength and opinionated non-superhero views to sympathize with clients and be there for her friends.

A FAMILY DEATH

During the Marvel Comics event *Civil War II*, Jen is knocked unconscious in battle and later falls into a coma. When she wakes up, she hasn't only changed mentally; she's also changed physically. Whereas before she could transform into She-Hulk and control herself, her other half is now untethered, triggered by her anger and trauma. Jen is forced to keep her rage at bay, and it's a loss in more ways than one—while transforming used to make her feel empowered, it now makes her upset because it reminds her of the emotional pain she experienced. She pulls away from her friends and locks herself in her apartment, plagued by thoughts that she can't control. She's irritable, uncontrolled, and dealing with panic attacks. She is plagued by PTSD-like symptoms, such as recurring and intrusive memories, along with overwhelming guilt due to the fact she couldn't save or say goodbye to Bruce Banner before he was killed in the same battle that almost took her own life. For Jen, becoming She-Hulk now brings rage and traumatic memories of her last fight and the friends and colleagues she's lost. "In addition to fear and anxiety, anger is a very common reaction to trauma," writes Seth Gillihan, PhD, in a *Psychology Today* article.[lxi] "We might feel anger at the person or situation responsible for our trauma. We may be angry at ourselves if we blame ourselves for what happened."

WORK AND TRAUMA

It's hard enough to overcome these emotional and mental road-blocks on our own, but it's even harder trying to deal with them while working a full-time job in a high-stress profession. In her most recent solo Marvel Comics series *Hulk*, Jen throws herself into work while trying to deal with her stress, attempting to establish some normalcy. She returns to her lawyer lifestyle, where she sur-rounds herself with coworkers and meets a new client named Maise, who is dealing with some of the same struggles Jen has been facing. With Maise, Jen sees an opportunity: she can't figure out how to help herself through her own trauma, but she might be able to help someone else through theirs.

Jen's first meeting with Maise ends in disaster, however, as Jen struggles with memories of her own trauma and almost hulks out in her panic.[lxii] The episode leaves her depressed, recovering alone as she tries to deal with its aftermath. This isn't the only time Jen experiences loss of control—for example, once triggered by a game of snowball in Central Park where children were re-enacting the events that put her in a coma, she couldn't contain her inner monster and ran back to her office to hide, smashing a few objects in the process.[lxiii] "Individuals who have PTSD can have very similar experiences to what She-Hulk struggles with, without 'hulking out,'" explains Dr. Saborsky. "Trauma survivors are often triggered emotionally and can experience irritability and trouble regulating the intense emotions they experience after a trauma. Per the DSM-5 [the American Psychiatric Association's *Diagnostic and Statistical Manual of Mental Disorders*, Fifth Edition], along with having irritability and aggression, those with trauma history can also have several risk-taking behaviors, a heightened startle reaction, and destructive behaviors, much like She-Hulk."

LEARNING FROM A HERO

Even though Jen sometimes rejects the people who want to help because they trigger her or stress her out, it's important to remember that we *can* ask for help, especially if we're going home each day and locking ourselves in our room, refusing to talk to anyone about our problems. Jen's best friend Patsy Walker (also known as the superhero

Hellcat) is insistent on connecting with Jen until she talks. Patsy shows us that it's a good idea to keep reaching out to friends going through trauma. She extends support to Jen, and even though Jen may not want it, knowing the option is there gives her a reason to reach out to her friend when she does feel okay.

If we do need to deal with struggles on our own, finding hobbies that are healthy and safe are a good way to distract our minds and help us refocus—Jen starts watching shows about baking, which helps her turn her brain off. While it's not healthy to push away our trauma and deny that it's a part of us, having an outlet like watching a favorite television show or listening to a favorite album can help take our mind off our troubles.

Superheroes are seen as powerful and confident beings, but sometimes being a superhero can take a toll on one's mental health. We see Jen address negative thoughts about herself and face memories that are difficult to process, but seeing mental health issues normalized in this way reminds us that even our heroes face issues they need to overcome.

I AM PROUD OF
WHO I AM

Sometimes our greatest strengths are more than just benefits. They are also our adversaries. We can be smart, we can be confident, and we can seem like we have everything under control. But that doesn't mean that these traits can't have a negative effect on us.

Categorized as "the brightest witch of her age," Hermione Granger comes to Hogwarts School of Witchcraft and Wizardry with a deep love of learning, an innate mastery of complex spells, and maturity beyond her years. Born to "**Muggle**" parents, Hermione had a different upbringing than most children. She had to be self-sufficient when it came to understanding spells and learning about the wizarding world at large, and she was responsible for teaching herself scholarly knowledge as well as practical knowledge in order to fit in with her new classmates. But Hermione's smarts weren't just a gift. Her perfectionism, drive for knowledge, and obsession with success

MUGGLE:
the slang term for someone who is not a witch or a wizard and has no natural magical abilities

made her talents potentially detrimental to not only her mental health but also her friends and family.

They were, in many ways, adversaries.

GENERALIZED ANXIETY DISORDER

Hermione is never diagnosed with a specific mental health issue, but many of her issues are similar to the symptoms of those who suffer from generalized anxiety disorder (GAD), one of the most common anxiety disorders. Generalized anxiety disorder tends to manifest in exaggerated thinking or constant dwelling on worst-case scenarios. For people who suffer from GAD, their focus on everything being terrible often leads to what psychologists call *catastrophizing*, where an individual assumes the worst possible scenario will occur.

"In the early books [of the *Harry Potter* series], Hermione appears to experience severe distress when it comes to schoolwork and performance. In fact, in her first year, her perfectionism initially caused a conflict between her, Ron, and Harry," says Dr. Scarlet. Hermione is not just obsessed with getting good grades; for a long time, she is hesitant to help her new friends Harry Potter and Ron Weasley and only does so when the situation is extremely dire—such as during their first year at Hogwarts, when she helps the duo take down a rogue cave troll. Despite the fact that Hermione becomes more willing to help her friends break rules over the years, she still constantly reprimands them, gets angry at Harry when he puts himself in danger, and pushes back against doing anything that could jeopardize her success at Hogwarts. In perhaps the biggest show of Hermione's obsession with her perfectionism, the third book in the series, *Harry Potter and the Prisoner of Azkaban*, has the students engaging in an exercise where they face a **boggart**. While some students see spiders or severed hands, Hermione sees a teacher who tells her she has failed all her exams. "Hermione is very similar to many of the teenagers I'm currently seeing, who are working to thrive in our competitive education system and to have the best grades and test scores," says Dr. Saborsky.

> **BOGGART:**
> a mystical, shapeshifting creature that materializes in the form most feared by its nearest adversary and which can be repelled only by laughter

NEGATIVE THOUGHTS AND SELF-DOUBT

Hermione doesn't just face criticism from her classmates because she's smart. Her Muggle-born status, combined with the fact she's a successful female, makes her a target for many who believe that only pureblood wizards should be able to succeed and thrive at Hogwarts. She is a frequent target of pureblood wizard Draco Malfoy, who taunts her and makes fun of her, while many other classmates make fun of her for being so scholarly. Hermione's passionate nature and strict views about how people should be treated lead her to spearhead the creation of the group **S.P.E.W.**, which protests the mistreatment of house elves. This paints her as a target yet again, though this time for racism, discrimination, and ridicule. Regardless, Hermione follows her instincts to protect magical creatures from discrimination, because she knows how it feels to be discriminated against herself.

> **S.P.E.W.:**
> the Society for the Promotion of Elfish Welfare

Always striving to be perfect, Hermione lives in fear of making mistakes and being wrong. Her fears visit her again in the final book of the series, *Harry Potter and the Deathly Hallows*. Hermione, Ron, and Harry must take turns wearing a locket cursed by the dark wizard Lord Voldemort. While under its influence, she finds that its powers cause her to question her own intellect, instilling her with self-doubt.

A *Psychology Today* article by Raj Raghunathan, PhD, suggests that "even though people claim to hold themselves in high regard, the thoughts that spontaneously occur to them—their 'mental chatter,' so to speak—is mostly (up to 70 percent) negative, a phenomenon that could be referred to as *negativity dominance*."[lxiv] The magic that Hermione comes into contact with while wearing the locket is similar to the influence of negative thoughts; sometimes we have dark voices that tell us we are not strong enough, smart enough, or brave enough. Sometimes we also get stuck in a cycle of negativity dominance, no matter how positive we are about other aspects of our life and no matter how much belief we have in ourselves based on our achievements.

LEARNING FROM A HERO

By the end of her time at Hogwarts, Hermione has successfully achieved confidence—but it isn't because she gets rid of her anxiety. It's because her anxiety has helped her overcome her own mental roadblocks when she learns how to channel it into something useful. According to Todd Kashdan and Robert Biswas-Diener, authors of *The Upside of Your Dark Side*, "Negative emotions like anxiety and suspiciousness can act like an attentional funnel that narrows the mind's eye to important details."[lxv] Because of Hermione's anxiety, she's more alert to danger, she's motivated to study harder, and she's constantly vigilant. In fact, the reason that Harry is able to successfully defeat Voldemort is in large part due to Hermione's resilience, which led her to obsessively study and learn about the wizarding world. And it's

Session Notes

"While [Hermione's] brain is a great asset and some of the skills and rigidity she has benefit the trio throughout *Harry Potter*, she could definitely use some flexibility to help her move forward in certain situations. With teens like Hermione, I usually teach them how to be flexible thinkers. We challenge their thoughts and decide whether they are accurate or helpful. If the thought isn't helpful, we find ways to 'defuse' the thought and make it just a thought and not so emotional.

"For example, I may have the teenager write their rigid thoughts down on paper and change the wording to 'I'm having the thought that . . .' Or they may do a meditation exercise that has them sending the thought away in some way, like on a leaf down a stream. I would also have Hermione practice using coping tools I teach her in situations that are out of her control and to try not to fight those situations so much, so that she 'rides the wave' of emotion that she will likely struggle with when she isn't doing things the way she typically does."

—Amy Saborsky, PsyD

Hermione's activism with S.P.E.W. that helps her become more comfortable in the face of discrimination from her classmates, which in turn helps her develop a stronger identity and stand up in the face of her anxiety and fears.

"As the series progress, Hermione still might be experiencing anxiety and perfectionism, however, it does not seem to be distressing for her, nor does it seem to intervene with her functioning. In this case, we could say that her anxiety is actually functional and is helping her meet her goals," says Dr. Scarlet. Hermione teaches us that we don't have to be hindered by the parts of us that we can't change—and this is what makes *her* the true hero of the wizarding world.

PRACTICING SELF-CARE: Lessons from Hermione Granger

If you asked her, Hermione Granger would likely be glad to sit down and teach you everything you need to know about Muggles, wizards, and potions. But history and spells aren't the only lessons Hermione can teach us. We can learn a lot from Hermione about overcoming our adversaries, and we don't even need to know how to use magic to do so.

1. **Allow yourself to be appreciated.** Understanding that you are more than what you achieve on a test can not only improve your attitude; it can also keep your self-standards from becoming toxic. Hermione's friends come to her for help with issues like romantic relationships, friendships, and family, which allows her to realize that even if she failed every test, her friends would still think of her as a valuable person in their lives.

2. **Put aside time for yourself.** When Hermione shows up at the Yule Ball, she doesn't look like she always does while running to class every day, and everyone notices how confident and happy she is. Whether it's a little bit of makeup or even just changing out of your sweatpants, breaking out of your comfort zone can drastically increase your confidence, energy, and happiness.

3. **Allow yourself to take breaks.** Even Hermione can't study all the time, and it's probably when she takes a nap, drinks some pumpkin juice, or takes a walk that the most brilliant inspiration (or the answer to a problem) strikes. Being able to recognize when you're working *too* hard and giving yourself a well-needed break is important so you don't burn out or fall into a toxic mindset.

real heroes _____

SAM MAGGS[lxvi]

@SAMMAGGS

Sam Maggs is the bestselling writer of comics, video games, and books such as *The Fangirl's Guide to the Galaxy, Wonder Women,* and *Girl Squads.* A writer for Insomniac Games and an on-air personality for geek-inspired shows like *Fangirling,* Sam is one of the community's leading authorities for women in pop culture.

Q: **Who is the female character that you identify with most when it comes to personal struggles, and why?**

A: Hermione Granger. I saw myself so much in her because I am a perfectionist with compulsive tendencies—something I read into her character. We experience so much pressure to be successful externally, but when that pressure is coming from the inside and there's no way to turn it off, things can get really difficult. I've been lucky to find cognitive behavioral therapy and to start to learn how to manage my anxiety disorder—I like to think Hermione probably did so eventually, too.

Q: **Why do you think we, as artists/individuals, identify so much with characters who have undergone mental health struggles, even though we know they're fictional?**

A: I think representation is important for everyone. We all need to see ourselves on the screen or on the page so that we can feel "normal" (whatever that means) and seen and understood. So that we know we're not alone. Characters with mental health struggles help to "normalize" [people with mental health struggles] in society. We should all be comfortable talking about mental health, and fiction gives us a great lens through which to do that.

Q: What have the female characters you've worked on in your creative endeavors taught you when it comes to overcoming your own obstacles?

A: That everyone has something going on that we don't know about. They might not have your thing, but they have their own thing. So I treat myself and others with more kindness.

Q: What advice can you give to people who might be struggling to find their own light in a dark place?

A: You're not alone—don't try to deal with it on your own! Professional help is invaluable. There are people trained to doctor your brain. Let them!

A CONVERSATION ABOUT
FICTIONAL CHARACTERS, MENTAL HEALTH, & SELF-CARE WITH
Dr. Andrea Letamendi

Q: In your work as both a licensed psychologist and a fan of pop culture, what has been your experience in terms of hearing from people who see themselves represented in certain fictional characters because of the way they deal with obstacles or mental health issues?

A: I think what's incredibly helpful and instrumental about fictional characters is that they do provide a very safe and welcoming space to create dialogue and to create critical conversations about issues like mental health, resilience, and wellness overall. In particular, the discussions around trauma, around recovery, around adversity, and around isolation are incredibly relevant, and when we witness and experience those kinds of narratives in fictional characters that we relate to, we do get a sense of validation. We do get a sense of support. And there's a strong sense of what's called *identification* with fictional characters. Identification is that very real sense of believability to a person, whether it's through their identity, through their experiences, through similar traumas, or through their narratives. I think a lot of people expect that we can identify with real people, real persons or figures that are in our lives, and I think fictional characters are often underestimated when it comes to the impact they have on us. They can be particularly powerful when it comes to emotional wellness and psychological recovery.

Q: You're well-known for consulting with comic writer Gail Simone on a few *Batgirl* issues, specifically the issues where Barbara Gordon enters therapy to deal with her trauma. Barbara's treatment is so important because it shows that it doesn't matter how super you are—everyone needs help, whether through therapy or medication or something else.

A: What Gail Simone did, which I think is a really important approach, is to have two comic issues that address Barbara Gordon's therapeutic relationship. The first one was when we meet her therapist and we get to know a little bit more about her treatment. The follow-up references to her therapist are a little more in passing, but we're reminded that therapy and psychological services are ongoing and dynamic and not a one-time thing. And I appreciated that perspective of demonstrating what a therapeutic process or therapist relationship might be like. There is the sense that Barbara Gordon sees herself as strong and resilient; she sees herself as someone who has grit and has to be the best that she can be. These are very relatable qualities for a lot of women, and yet sometimes that level of needing to be perfect, needing to be reliable for everybody, needing to be the best, can be detrimental to her well-being.

I think in her journey, she has self-doubt, she has imposter syndrome, she has those negative thoughts that kind of creep in. We realize that she's not perfect, and we realize that she has vulnerabilities that are very real. The amazing part about her [story] arc with the villain she stands up against is that it's incredibly important to her story, because the common thread is "are you going to be as strong and as powerful as you want to be as a superhero?" And you're reminded of your failures or vulnerabilities. I think for a lot of us, this is really difficult to address—how can we be our better self, how can we recover from our traumas if we're constantly reminded of the ways in which we either failed someone else or failed ourselves? It has a lot of weight on us. It's difficult to overcome. With the help of a professional practitioner, there is hope. There is a sense that the hard work she puts into [therapy] is valuable and has a good outcome, and I really appreciate that in the writing.

Q: A number of women profiled in *Geek Girls Don't Cry* deal with the "hero" aspect of being constantly in the spotlight. Wonder Woman is perhaps the most well-known when it comes to having that kind of public persona, but she's also someone who has an immense amount of compassion.

A: At first blush, it seems she's infallible and so super that she's kind of unreachable. I really think that Gal Gadot's version of her gives us a little more of that humanity, that compassion that reminds us that there are some qualities about this character that we can relate to. I appreciate your perspective of what's underneath some of the front-facing characteristics of that persona of being every woman. What *is* that pressure to be every woman? You have to be everything. You have to be compassionate, you have to be strong, you have to be attractive, you have to be desirable, you have to be successful, you have to be alert, you have to be ten other things on a daily basis. Appreciating Wonder Woman's plight when it comes to that perspective and both her ability to encompass all these characteristics and feel the pressure to maintain—that is really valuable. It reminds us of the ways in which we may feel that intensity or that pressure.

So how do we turn a little bit more inward and think about what we're giving to others—whether it's help, whether it's our persona, whether it's our presence—when can we turn inward and think about what our needs are? And when we do have that time for reflection, that time for self-care and self-soothing? And for everybody, it's going to be a little different, but I think [Wonder Woman] can help us address, in really meaningful ways, how to have those moments of self-reflections and self-care. I think it's that interesting duality of having that strong sense of self, of having that sense of confidence and knowing our abilities well, and I think, as women, when we reach that self-actualization, it's really meaningful for us. We hold on to that sense of confidence. But that duality is, when do we allow ourselves to be more vulnerable? When do we allow ourselves to make mistakes, and not only make those mistakes but forgive ourselves for making those mistakes? That's where that self-compassion comes in. [Wonder Woman] is really helpful because her compassion is, yes, a lot of times directed at other people, but I think we can turn that direction inward. That's not too far from where she is.

Q: The concept of found family—essentially, a group of people unrelated to you but who support you and are important to your self-care—is a common thread that ties many of these characters together, especially when it comes to moving past their obstacles. In my opinion, *Firefly*'s River Tam is probably one of the most classic examples of how important found family is for people struggling with mental health issues.

A: One of the strongest predictors of recovery and moments after a traumatic experience is social support, and I think [River Tam's experience] is a really good demonstration of how the people around her are supportive. They are receptive to her, and there's a little bit of meeting her where she's at. There's a little bit of compromising for her, but not in a bad way. There's an openness for how she is and there's an immense amount of understanding for her. That empathy piece is really important. *We don't all need to know exactly what you went through, but we care about you and we don't want you to be triggered. We don't want you to be in an unsafe space ever again, so we'll do what we can to meet your needs.* Having said that, there's also a little bit of direction of pushing her toward growth. She can't be like this forever. She can't be frozen in her post-traumatic grief or post-traumatic sense of self, so there is a little bit of pushing her toward wellness by challenging her just a little bit. By virtue of being a part of this community, she is being asked to grow toward recovery, to develop a little more, and we all need that.

We all can't stay frozen in [our] trauma. We all need to do work and development toward healing so we find ourselves in a better place.

Q: **Who is a character that you relate to—someone who has helped you through a difficult time, or someone who has particular meaning for you?**

A: I probably could list ten women! I think for me, Rey's journey in *Star Wars* [Episodes VII and VIII] is really, really impactful. A part of that was her learning about her history from Kylo Ren—that part is not as important to me, but [what was important were] the sense of all these expectations about who you're supposed to be and where you come from and how your history is supposed to tell everyone else what your journey is. And as a comment that she's from nobody, that she's nothing, those comments are both painful and kind of inspiring. Because it reminded me of why *Star Wars* was one of the first fanships that I developed: the ideas that you really could see yourself as a person who is seemingly from nothing and unimportant and realize that you could have your own journey that you decide. You can have your own journey that you are controlling and you feel a sense of empowerment. It doesn't really matter who my parents are, where I came from, or what I'm supposed to do. I can overcome those hardships with my own resilience and my own resources or my own ideas. So that sense of independence and self-ownership . . . those are the qualities that, for me, I was really inspired by when it comes to Rey.

Part Four

OVERCOMING
DEPRESSION

Depression likes to tell us many lies: that we don't have a place in this world, that our thoughts are not worth anything, and that we'll never be able to make a difference. Depression is, in many ways, a monster that tries to bully us into thinking we can't succeed in what we want to do—or be who we want to be.

According to a PubMed study, "Depression is the leading cause of disease-related disability in women. Epidemiological studies have shown that the lifetime prevalence of a major depressive disorder in women (21.3 percent) is almost twice that in men (12.7 percent)."[lxvii] All the women in the following chapters have experienced debilitating traumatic experiences that have caused them to suffer depression. Jessica Jones deals with an abusive relationship, B'Elanna Torres deals with self-harm and the loss of her found family, Supergirl deals with being a world's icon in the face of personal loss, Scarlet Witch deals with the pressure of her superpowers, and Juliet Burke deals with being physically and emotionally secluded. With the help of people who believe in them and their own resilience, these women push through the barriers of depression and show the world they are more than what their mental health tries to say they are.

THE PRIVATE EYE

For people who experience abuse or traumatic situations that lead to depression, the road to recovery—especially for women—is long and sometimes slow. According to the American Psychological Association, "Although women are at greater risk for negative consequences following traumatic events, many often hesitate to seek mental health treatment. Survivors often wait years to receive help, while others never receive treatment at all."[lxviii]

While Marvel character Jessica Jones is a survivor, the street-smart hero isn't just known for her physical strength. Anything good that Jessica has experienced has come with a price, success going hand in hand with tragedy. She acquires superpowers as a teenager but at the expense of a terrible accident that places her in a coma and kills her entire family. She becomes a superhero due to those powers, but her life is derailed by an abusive boyfriend who emotionally tortures her and uses her powers as a weapon to hurt others. Every time Jessica undergoes another moment of trauma that affects her mental health, it's her psychological resilience that helps her triumph.

KILGRAVE'S INFLUENCE

Statistics state that "one in three young people experience physical or sexual abuse in their romantic relationship" and that "young people who experience dating abuse are at risk for disordered eating, lower grades, PTSD, depression, and suicide."[lxix] Jessica meets fellow superhuman Zebediah Kilgrave when he sees her displaying her superhuman strength. Immediately taken by her powers and looks, Kilgrave asks Jessica to dinner, beginning their relationship together. To Jessica, Kilgrave seems like the perfect boyfriend—he shows her the attention she's been craving, he treats her like a queen, and he gives her the stability that she's looking for in her otherwise rocky life. But their relationship quickly goes downhill when Kilgrave begins manipulating her, forcing her to use her powers to take actions that she normally wouldn't. It takes awhile for Jessica to free herself from Kilgrave both psychologically and physically, and when she does, she's left traumatized, constantly haunted by nightmares and flashbacks. Her trauma and depression manifest themselves in specific yet poignant ways: she becomes overly vigilant, she uses vices like alcohol to numb her pain, and she stays far away from anything associated with her former life, including friends, as well as physical locations where abuse occurred.

Jessica's experience is not only a stark example of women who have been abused and manipulated, it is an example of emotional abuse, driving home the knowledge that more people are susceptible to this kind of trauma than we might realize. According to the National Domestic Violence Hotline, roughly 10.7 percent of women have been stalked and almost half of the women in the US have experienced psychological aggression from an intimate partner.[lxx]

Even though Kilgrave has mind-control powers, he only uses those powers for a brief time with Jessica, instead choosing to control a majority of their relationship the same way that many abusers do: by not letting her out of his sight, making sure she does what he wants, playing the victim when she does something to upset him or anger him, and manipulating her to believe that she is doing everything out of her own will. When Jessica escapes Kilgrave's clutches and tries to rebuild her life, she is still haunted by him—hearing his voice, seeing him on the streets, or being reminded of his presence at certain restaurants. In the eighth episode of the first season of the Netflix® series *Jessica Jones*, when Kilgrave has been brought back into Jessica's life, he convinces Jessica to return to her childhood home with him. He pretends to put her in control by letting her dictate their pretend relationship—a technique many abusers use to lure survivors back into their grasp.

DISSOCIATION

Although Jessica's dissociation is never specifically labeled, her behavior fits the characteristics for what psychologists call *psychogenic fugue*, which is defined as "memory loss characteristic of amnesia, loss of one's identity, and fleeing from one's home environment."[lxxi] Thanks to Kilgrave's abuse, Jessica feels like she does not know who she is anymore; she is certainly not the person she was before she met him, and she is also a different person because of her powers.

Whether they are brought on by triggers or whether they simply appear in everyday life due to the trauma she's endured, Jessica exhibits a range of dissociative episodes. She is woken up from her dreams with memories of Kilgrave harassing her; she sees people who have similar profiles or who wear similar clothing when she's out on the street; and she can't look away from instances of mugging and fighting because it reminds her of what Kilgrave made her do when she was under his control. To deal with these episodes, Jessica combats her dissociation by grounding herself—a common technique psychologists use on their patients to tether them to reality. In Jessica's case, she repeats street names from her childhood when her trauma-related memories manifest.

LEARNING FROM A HERO

Like Xena the Warrior Princess and Princess Leia Organa, Jessica finds a purpose that allows her to move forward: helping others. When she hears that other women have been abused by Kilgrave, she starts taking action to ensure that he can't hurt anyone else the same way he's hurt her. In the Netflix series, Jessica comes across a therapy group for people who have been abused by Kilgrave. Jessica is steadfastly independent, righteous, and believes that she doesn't need anyone to help her, especially when it comes to her trauma. But when she finds the aforementioned support group and befriends a neighbor who is also struggling with his own issues, she realizes she doesn't have to go through her traumas alone. Speaking out about the past can be scary, because doing so has the potential to invite the memory of abusers back into our life. But speaking out can also help us realize that we are not alone, and we can help others by allowing people to know our secrets.

Although Jessica possesses the powers of a superhero, she is reluctant to become one. She feels like she can barely take care of herself to begin with, and when she does try to fight past her trauma, she puts other people in danger, even though it's unintentional. It's clear why Jessica thinks she doesn't have credibility to be a hero, much less someone qualified to save others. But because Jessica doesn't let her depression pull her down and because she chooses to face her fears and step forward, she *becomes* a hero—our hero—whether she wants to wear the mantle or not.

THE ENGINEER

Clinical depression can have many different causes: a genetic family history, difficult situational life events, negative thinking patterns . . . or gender.

B'Elanna Torres stands out in pop culture as one of the smartest and strongest *Star Trek* characters. Not only is she a competent female engineer, she's proficient in combat, confident in her actions, loyal, fierce, and intelligent. Below the surface, however, is a version of B'Elanna that we don't necessarily know about: the one who suffers from deep clinical depression as diagnosed in the episode "Extreme Risk," the one who dealt with anxiety and insecurity from an early age, and the one who constantly battles with her mental health.[lxxii]

GROWING UP WITH INSECURITIES

B'Elanna has always dealt with identifying in two different ways: as a human and as a **Klingon**, since her parents were of different races. While that

> **KLINGON:**
> fictional humanoid species in *Star Trek*

connection is shown in her looks, her personality is also defined by the different parts of her heritage. As a Klingon, she's moody and angry, and as a human, she's considerably more docile and demure.

B'Elanna's experience growing up is similar to what children of mixed races or different cultures often experience: she's teased for her different looks and feels alienated from everyone around her. This insecurity hits her at an early age because she and her mother are the only Klingons on a planet of humans. It becomes more prominent in the *Star Trek: Voyager* season 7 episode "Lineage," when the adult B'Elanna recalls feeling like her father was distancing himself because B'Elanna was embracing more of her mother's Klingon behavior.[lxxiii] When he left B'Elanna and her mother, she was only five years old, and she believed that she was the reason her father abandoned them. She never talks about these feelings, however—they stay locked up inside of her, festering over the years and taking a toll on her mental health. Breaking down the five types of guilt and how to cope with them, Dr. Whitbourne writes for *Psychology Today*, "as cognitive theories of emotions tell us, much of the unhappiness we experience is due to our own irrational thoughts about situations."[lxxiv] An example of this can be seen when describing the feeling of guilt you might feel for something you *think* you did wrong—in the case of B'Elanna, she thinks she made her father leave because she didn't show the "correct" side of her personality.

In the same episode, B'Elanna finds herself pregnant and having the revelation that her daughter may be born with the same hybrid features, which brings up the memories of her father's abandonment, her insecurities, and her childhood anxiety. She acts erratically and puts the health and well-being of her unborn child at risk, proving that the memories haven't disappeared. They are still there, waiting to be brought out by a trigger or a negative thought. "People like B'Elanna, who are bullied at a young age for being different, might become very sensitive to criticism and rejection," says Dr. Scarlet. "Furthermore, people whose parents abandon them in the way that B'Elanna's father abandoned her might also become fearful of further rejection by others. In some cases, the individual may engage in aggressive behaviors or become withdrawn when fearing further rejection."

DEPRESSION: The Real Monster

In the *Star Trek: Voyager* season five episode "Extreme Risk," B'Elanna is diagnosed with clinical depression by the ship's doctor. Although she struggles with different mental health issues throughout her life, B'Elanna's clinical depression begins when she learns about the death of her **Maquis** friends, who have been murdered. At this point, B'Elanna feels like she's lost everything. She had discovered a home and found family in the Maquis, but knowing that they are now gone, B'Elanna feels like she has lost the last people who cared about her and the only family she had ever really known.

MAQUIS: a paramilitary group made up of rebellious colonists and Starfleet officers

Following this loss, B'Elanna feels numb. She resorts to self-harm, trying to injure herself both around the ship and on her own in order to feel something. According to the National Alliance of Mental Illness, "The urge to hurt yourself may start with overwhelming anger, frustration or pain. . . . Sometimes, injuring yourself stimulates the body's endorphins or pain-killing hormones, thus raising their mood. Or if a person doesn't feel many emotions, he might cause himself pain in order to feel something 'real' to replace emotional numbness."[lxxv]

B'Elanna self-harms in order to find a "quick fix" because she's concerned that she doesn't feel any emotion for the tragedy she's experienced. But this crutch of self-harm soon spirals, as B'Elanna begins using it whenever she needs a reminder that she should feel the pain that she's dealing with. Her friend Commander Chakotay rightfully assesses that B'Elanna self-harms because she's scared to feel something—fearing that once she allows herself to unleash her emotions, she won't be able to control them.

According to the National Institute of Mental Health's 2015 booklet on depression, "Not everyone who is depressed experiences every symptom. Some people experience only a few symptoms. Some people have many. The severity and frequency of symptoms, and how long they last, will vary depending on the individual and his or her particular illness."[lxxvi] For B'Elanna, her depression causes her insecurities to return. She becomes reclusive, pulls back from her work, and becomes withdrawn. She doesn't seem to find joy in anything—even in eating food that she loved as a child—and her attitude changes; she snaps at her friends and doesn't seem to be engaged in her work, becoming uncharacteristically erratic.

LEARNING FROM A HERO

When Captain Janeway realizes that B'Elanna is exhibiting unusual behavior, such as a detachment in her work and a more subdued personality, she immediately becomes concerned and sends someone to check on her friend. And it is Commander Chakotay who helps B'Elanna realize that, even though she feels like her family is gone, she has a new family in the USS *Voyager* crew—and they won't abandon her.

Chakotay also convinces B'Elanna that she should be the one to fix an issue on the ship when it comes under attack, even though doing so will mean that she has to face the memories she's been running from and the demons that sparked her depression in the first place. Sometimes you need to go back to your roots to try to find some normalcy. B'Elanna came to the USS *Voyager* with the skills and expertise that made her the chief engineer, and taking back control by returning to a skill she knows helps her gain confidence, refocus, and put things back in perspective so that she can start to heal.

THE IDOL

The hard truth is that, as women, we are given more expectations than men. We are expected to do more for the family, we are expected to do more at work, and we are expected to prove ourselves. So it's not surprising that, according to Mental Health America, more women experience depression than men. "While the reasons for this are still unclear, they may include the hormonal changes women go through during menstruation, pregnancy, childbirth, and menopause. Other reasons may include the stress caused by the multiple responsibilities that women have."[lxxvii]

As Supergirl, Kara Danvers's most notable power is her strength—and for good reason. She's able to lift tons of steel, she can shoot lasers out of her eyes, and she can fly. Debuting in 1959's *Action Comics* #252, Kara is one of DC's notable female superheroes.[lxxviii] When she was given her own television show to headline in 2015, it was refreshing to see a focus on a female character who wasn't just physically strong but who also dealt with the very human struggle of trying to fit in as an outsider. We identify with women like Kara because they exhibit powerful abilities, but it's more powerful that we can see them feel weak or struggle with their feelings and still triumph.

YOUNG AND ALONE

In season two of the CW Network® television series *Supergirl*, Kara experiences grief when she resigns herself to the final loss of her first true love, Mon-El, who enters a vortex that leads to an unknown fate. In season three, she experiences the jolt of anxiety and confusion that comes with Mon-El's return—his journey landed him in the future, where he lived for seven years along with a new love. And she experiences betrayal when an evil superhero takes over her friend's mind and almost fatally injures her. With all of this weighing on Kara in addition to being responsible for the safety of the world, it's not surprising that she falls into a state of depression. "Stress has direct effects on mood, and early initial symptoms of lowered mood can include irritability, sleep disruption, and cognitive changes such as impaired concentration," says published author and researcher Alice Boyes, PhD, on *Psychology Today*. "However, the indirect effects of stress are often what causes depression to take hold. . . . When people experience stress, they often stop doing some of the healthy coping strategies that usually help keep their mood on track."[lxxix]

It's also important to remember that Kara arrived on Earth later than she should have. Her pod was knocked off course after escaping Krypton, and by the time Kara made it to Earth, her cousin Kal-El had already grown up and become Superman. Essentially, he had done the work that she was meant to do, and now Kara was left to inherit the patriarchy—a sizable amount of pressure for anyone but especially for a young girl who has come to a strange planet with no family and with powers that she has to hide. While she's portrayed as strong and resilient, it's not a surprise that her mental health issues eventually take a toll on her.

RED KRYPTONITE

During *Supergirl*'s first season episode "Falling," Kara is exposed to a substance called Red Kryptonite.[lxxx] Unlike Green Kryptonite, which makes people from Krypton lose their strength, Red Kryptonite causes weakness in other ways—namely, through a dramatic personality shift. After being exposed to Red Kryptonite, Kara becomes irritable and negative, blowing off her work duties and snapping at her friends. Like Lord Voldemort's locket acting as a metaphor for Hermione Granger's negative thoughts, the Red Kryptonite can be seen as a metaphor for Kara's depression. In one of the episode's final scenes, Kara mentions that her brain was "altered." Kara wasn't a different person when she was under the influence of the Red Kryptonite, and she wasn't mind-controlled or brainwashed. She was simply Kara in a bad headspace—Kara in the throes of depression, like so many of us deal with.

The scariest part of depression can be the damage we do to ourselves and others when our brains are altered in the way Kara's was. After Kara becomes free of the Red Kryptonite, she becomes aware of the horrible things she's said and done—and she owns up to them. She doesn't say that they weren't her; instead, she admits they *were* her thoughts and feelings, just magnified in a negative way. She's aware of how badly she's hurt people, and she knows she can't pretend she wasn't aware of it, but she also knows she can start to heal by trying to own up to her actions.

LEARNING FROM A HERO

"Kara most likely struggles with having a good work-life balance," says Dr. Saborsky. "When we are around others and have to uphold a certain standard, it can take a toll on us physically and mentally. If Kara finds ways to continue to have self-care on her own, finds ways to achieve behavioral activation (the idea that we are happier beings when we are moving in some way), and is able to work on ways to disconnect, she would have much better mental health than the individual characterized in *Supergirl*."

We often don't want to talk about our mental health issues. Why? Because we think it'll show the world we're not strong and that we're giving up on fighting. Or maybe we just don't want to admit that we have a bigger problem than we realize. Moving forward isn't easy, but it's not impossible. As Kara shows us, *nothing* is impossible. And if Supergirl can do it, so can we.

PRACTICING SELF-CARE:
Lessons from Kara Danvers

Kara Danvers (or as she's known on her home planet, Kara Zor-El) is technically an alien, but she's had to overcome some pretty human issues. Here's what we can learn about self-care from Kara, aka Supergirl.

1. **Reinvent yourself and embrace her.** Kara knows she can never return to her old life. On Earth, Kara is a new person. But once she embraces her superpowers, her alien outsider feelings,

and her new unique life, she finds she's more comfortable with her personality. Focusing on your present life instead of a life you miss can help you become more optimistic and keep you positive about the future.

2. **Live life according to your own beliefs.** Kara doesn't let other people's opinions get in the way of what she knows is important: saving the world. Even though her friends and family sometimes disagree with her, she follows her instincts and lives life on her own terms, which helps her achieve her goals. Staying true to what you believe strengthens your confidence.

3. **Be proactive in helping others, physically and emotionally.** Once Kara starts owning her Supergirl mantle and saving people, her mood improves, because she is undertaking physical activity and also making a difference with her actions. Volunteering your time for something like a community service project can help improve your outlook and raise your spirits.

THE SORCERESS

Depression doesn't have to be sadness, and anxiety doesn't have to show itself with hand-wringing or panic attacks. "Depression doesn't always 'present' as it should," says Alice Walton, PhD, in *Forbes*. "Prolonged sadness, lack of hope, or loss of interest in previously enjoyed activities are the most commonly mentioned symptoms on mental health websites and in antidepressant ads, and they can certainly be the most affecting. But sometimes the disorder is subtler, and harder to identify, since it can make itself known in stranger ways than we'd like."[lxxxi]

When we look at Wanda Maximoff in her many comic runs as Scarlet Witch or in the Marvel Cinematic Universe® movies, we don't necessarily think of her as a woman with depression. Like Black Widow, Wanda is strong, powerful, and considered both an Avenger and a hero. And like Black Widow, her comics history has provided her with numerous retcons and retellings. But one story has remained constant—her struggles with mental health and how she's had to learn to deal with her superpowers.

HIDING EMOTIONS

Abandoned at birth, Wanda and her twin brother, Pietro, were raised by different individuals throughout their childhood—including Magneto, the X-Men-turned-villainous-leader of the Brotherhood of Mutants. It was likely this untethered upbringing, along with the death of their parents, which led to Wanda's quest for emotional stability. According to a study referenced in an article from students at Vanderbilt University, "Investigating the connection between parent's investment and children's competence suggests that the emotional involvement of parents really does matter and affects the outcome of their child's emotional competence and regulation."[lxxxii]

Wanda demonstrates this need for emotional stability by constantly trying to connect herself to people who can take care of her. In 1964's *The X-Men* #4, she attaches herself to her brother Quicksilver and her close teammate Hawkeye, hoping to find a foundation for her feelings and emotions with another person who understands her.[lxxxiii] But Wanda's mental health proves to be a bigger obstacle than she realizes, as neither are the right match; Quicksilver is too protective, while Hawkeye is too aggressive. When Wanda falls in love with the android Vision, eventually marrying him in 1974's *Giant-Size Avengers* #4, it's not hard to see why she's chosen him.[lxxxiv] Vision is logical and controlled, and because he is a sentient human, he has emotional distance. Wanda feels safe with Vision, whereas other men in her life were too reactionary for her anxiety.

MAGIC AND MENTAL HEALTH

As a mutant, Wanda possesses powerful magic: she's able to use powers of telekinesis, hexing, and mind control. But being able to warp reality isn't so good for someone who struggles with their mental health, and despite her special skills, Wanda remains scared of her own powers and misunderstood by the world.

Wanda's mental instabilities have always been a part of her. She has been controlled and manipulated at every turn of her life, and it's no wonder that she suffers from depression relating to her powers. In the 2016 Marvel movie *Captain America: Civil War*, Wanda is on a mission with her team when she accidentally destroys a building that, in turn, kills hundreds of innocent people. It's not long before the government starts labeling her as a dangerous threat. Wanda retreats following this incident; she accepts being put under house arrest without protest and lets her own insecurities take over because she doesn't believe people will protect her or care about her.

"I have several clients who regularly deal with the issues Scarlet Witch deals with. They struggle with low self-esteem, so they try to put up a front that they are okay so that they are not asked about this or have to face their true emotions," says Dr. Saborsky. "We work in sessions to try and get that patient to feel as if they can be themselves, see that they have positive qualities, and that there is no reason to put up a facade for the people they care about. We work on ways to process their emotions about themselves and find ways to practice being themselves around others in a safe way, which helps their self-esteem grow and prevents them from not being true to others and themselves."

LEARNING FROM A HERO

Wanda repeatedly attempts to get help for her mental health issues. In her most recent solo comic series written by James Robinson, she studies with a witch named Agatha Harkness to understand her powers and how they affect her. She also turns to medication for help, outwardly telling Agatha that she has depression and mentioning in conversation that she can't accept an offered alcoholic drink because she is taking antidepressants.[lxxxv] While medication has long had a stigma, there have been numerous pushes to end that stigma so that more people can come forward and not feel ashamed of needing something more than a therapist when they are looking for help—and Wanda Maximoff is giving society one more push in the right direction.

In various comic stories throughout the years, Wanda also leaves the Avengers for a period of time to be on her own. In doing so, she takes the step of making her own well-being and health a priority—something that is important for us to realize we can do, even if we feel like we have a responsibility to be there for others. While letting people help us *is* sometimes the right thing to do, prioritizing our happiness—even if it means being alone—is also important. And there is no better person to remind us of that than a powerful hero.

THE DOCTOR

We don't get to pick the paths that we want to take in life, but we can try to approach those paths with positivity and optimism. However, we may not have a plan for when life doesn't fall into place the way we expect it to. *Adjustment disorder*, often referred to as *situational depression*, "often occurs with one or more of the following: depressed mood, anxiety, disturbance of conduct (in which the patient violates rights of others or major age-appropriate societal norms or rules), and maladaptive reactions (i.e. problems related to work or school, physical complaints, social isolation)."[lxxxvi]

A sharp and brilliantly talented fertility specialist, Juliet Burke never expected to experience adjustment disorder, and she never thought she'd end up living and working on an island in the middle of nowhere while essentially being held prisoner against her will. But she also never thought she'd face abusive relationships, the continuous loss of loved ones, and forced seclusion. Despite being thrown the biggest curveballs, Juliet learns how to find her strength. She uses that strength in order to become resilient and to become a survivor—in every sense of the word.

ADJUSTMENT DISORDER

According to *Psychology Today*, "the cause of adjustment disorder is a life stressor. In adults, adjustment disorder is commonly a result of stressors related to marital discord, finances, or work. In adolescents, common stressors include school problems, family or parents' marital problems, or issues around sexuality. Other types of stressors include the death of a loved one, life changes, unexpected catastrophes, and medical conditions such as cancer and subsequent treatments."[lxxxvii] Even before Juliet was recruited to work at the research facility on the island due to her exceptional talent, she was suffering from depression thanks to life events like her parents' divorce and her sister's battle with cancer. Growing up in the shadow of trauma, Juliet's desperation to belong to someone and find a home mirrors Wanda Maximoff's search for emotional stability. When Juliet meets her husband Edmund Burke through her research, everything seems too good to be true. But Edmund soon shows his true colors; he sees Juliet's natural talent as something to exploit and becomes more interested in using her to further his own career. For three years, Juliet endures his emotional abuse, leaving her stripped of her pride, personality, and confidence.

EMOTIONAL ABUSE

Although Juliet's relationship with Edmund isn't quite as violent as Jessica Jones's relationship with Kilgrave, she undergoes the same trauma that Jessica faced in the aftermath of being controlled by someone. Even though Juliet knew Edmund was a bad influence on her and her career, part of the reason she stayed with him was because Edmund tapped into those feelings of attachment and preyed on Juliet's biggest vulnerability: she just wanted someone to love her. Similarly, when Juliet meets Benjamin Linus, a longtime occupant and "leader" of the island to which Juliet is recruited, he attempts to win over her trust, allowing her to believe that she has finally found a true friend. But Ben, like Edmund, uses her for his own gain, exploiting her research skills and isolating her from her family. "People who get caught in the web of a controlling person are no different from others," writes Lisa Aronson Fontes, PhD, in her *Psychology Today* article "When Relationship Abuse Is Hard to Recognize." "They just have the bad luck to become involved with an abuser at a time when they are especially vulnerable. Typically, an abuser will lavish attention on a woman at the beginning of the relationship. Over time, he becomes jealous, monitors her whereabouts, and restricts her interactions with others."[lxxxviii] Ben's actions become so abusive that when he finds out that there's a man named Goodwin Stanhope, who Juliet has taken a legitimate interest in and become attracted to, he devises a plan to send him away. And when Juliet realizes that she's lost yet another close friend, her depression hits hard and she closes herself off.

LEARNING FROM A HERO

Although Juliet feels mostly alone due to her adjustment disorder, one ability allows her to begin overcoming her depression and low feelings of self-worth: being able to focus on her work. By doing the work she knows she is capable of, Juliet regains control over her situation, allowing her to put her own life back in focus. We see much of Juliet's life before she came to the island through flashbacks, and in the past, she is meek, shy, and hesitant. When we meet her in the present time, she is hardened, calm, and in control—showing that she has overcome her years of depression to reclaim her life. Juliet is not just a survivor: her resilience allows her to exercise judgment over her actions in order to gain control of her identity, which leads her to find a life that she's happy with—and one that finally allows her to be in control of her own narrative.

CATRINA DENNIS[lxxxix]

@OHCATRINA

Catrina Dennis is a journalist, narrative designer, podcaster, and producer. She is the creator of the webcomic *Treasure in the Core*, and co-hosts *Y Tu Bantha También*, a *Star Wars*–themed podcast with a Latinx lean. Catrina is also the assistant producer of *Looking for Leia*, a docuseries about *Star Wars* fandom history through the lens of the women who built it.

Q: Who is the female character that you identify with most when it comes to personal struggles, and why?

A: Right now, I can't stop thinking about Asajj Ventress from [animated television series] *Star Wars: The Clone Wars*. Her trauma and the way she deals with it aren't identical to my experiences (of course), but so often she falls and genuinely feels defeat. But then she gets up, even when she doesn't *want* to, and carves a path forward.

I think I relate to Ventress because she rose from a horrific, dark place and never genuinely gave up, but it was only when she allowed herself to truly process her feelings—the abandonment, the failure, and the fact that she had survived decades of abuse—that she began to flourish into this amazing, badass bounty hunter who opted not to kill when she didn't have to. Ventress wasn't perfect, but she looked at the problems that poisoned her mind and realized that she could handle them when she let herself understand them. She started following the paths that life gave her rather than desperately clinging to options that didn't work out.

So I guess that's it: Ventress reminds me that no matter how bad things get, I always have the option to choose the better route and to process my feelings so that I can understand them more clearly.

Q: **Why do you think we, as artists/individuals, identify so much with characters who have undergone mental health struggles, even though we know they're fictional?**

A: Representation is powerful, especially when it can be used as a tool to better understand what's happening to you personally. Whether the character is a hero, a villain, or just someone trying to get by, being able to see someone surviving with the same illnesses as you do is therapeutic. I also just think it's important to acknowledge that these problems are real, especially in fiction, where so many of us with mental illnesses turn to escape and feel validated as heroes or our favorite characters.

Q: **What have the female characters you've worked on in your creative endeavors taught you when it comes to overcoming your own obstacles?**

A: I've been very lucky as of recent to work on several amazing fictional women for upcoming projects. I keep going back to this, but I've learned how to survive because of women both fictional and real, so a lot of the women who inspire me in real life are in my characters in some way or another. My comic *Treasure in the Core* and my upcoming game *El Caleuche* are both led by Latinas who are in the process of learning how to deal with some large personal struggles. It's important, I think, that even though the characters might be in space (or at a party in the afterlife) they still have realistic struggles. Not only for the narrative but for the audience and the writer, too. Creating characters for my stories has helped me sort out a few problems I didn't know I had. You see them struggling with things that I think are relatable, like facing your failures or learning how to process your feelings in a safe and healthy way, and I think that's been beneficial for me and for the small audience I've shared them with.

Q: **What advice can you give to people who might be struggling to find their own light in a dark place?**

A: It's not wrong to look at your fictional heroes, or even major villains, and find yourself in them or to use your passion for these stories in order to work out your problems whenever you can't reach help. The fact that you're fighting this in any way is a wonderful sign and kind of a badge of honor, in my opinion. It means you know that something is wrong, and that, for me, is power—you're already out here proving that you're strong enough to face the monster by pointing at its face and calling it what it is. *You're gonna be okay.*

Part Five

OVERCOMING ISOLATION

Isolation doesn't necessarily have to fall under the common umbrella of not being surrounded by others. Isolation can come from disconnection with our peers or from simply losing someone close to us, either in death or by forcible means. An article from Harvard Medical School says that "loneliness is almost as prevalent as obesity," though we would be hard-pressed to look at individuals in the world and know offhand how many are truly suffering from isolation.[xc]

Perhaps that's why every female character in this section is so inspirational. River Tam was isolated by the government, Ellie was isolated by an apocalyptic outbreak, Cersei Lannister was isolated by societal norms, Rogue was isolated by her powers, and Buffy was isolated by her fate. All of these women experienced isolation in a way that affected their mental health—and all of them overcame the issues they struggled against, proving that they are worthy of being our heroes.

ALONE IN SPACE

To be gifted in any way, but especially as a child, means that more than just advanced intellect plays a role in a young individual's development. River Tam was just a child when she was enrolled in "the Academy," which was similar to Natasha Romanoff's Red Room—a place that promised to reward child prodigies but that in reality functioned as an abusive torture center. Instead of being nurtured to improve her smarts and skills, River's brain was experimented on by the government, leaving her in an unstable mental state. By the time River is rescued, she exhibits all the mental health issues of someone who has been abused, tortured, and isolated. And while we're shown how mentally unstable River is throughout her arc on Joss Whedon's television series *Firefly*, we're also shown how, even when it seems like nothing can be fixed, hope—and strength—can always find a way to guide us home.

TRAUMA, EMOTIONS, AND ISOLATION

While River's mental health issues are clearly attributed to the experimentation that she experienced, her isolation from her family and society didn't help. Even in today's world, there are instances where young children are taken from their parents against their will (at an age much younger than River) and put in unfamiliar surroundings while being separated them from their families—the 2018 border crisis and the disappearance of undocumented children being just one example.

According to a study on severe trauma and self-care structure, "Severe trauma affects all structures of the self—one's image of the body; the internalized images of the others; and one's values and ideals—and leads to a sense that the self-coherence and self-continuity are invaded, assaulted, and systematically broken down."[xci] As the study explains, sometimes a traumatic event is so strong that it becomes second nature, overtaking the body's natural responses to emotions or events like terror and catastrophe.

After recovering from her imprisonment, River struggles with trying to understand her emotions again, as the experiments done on her brain have left her in a near-psychotic state. River not only loses her mind, she loses her sense of self, which isolates her entirely. Even worse, she no longer gets to choose when she feels emotions, because she feels everything all the time. Thanks to what has been done to her, River now carries the emotional weight of everyone around her, including all of her Firefly crew members. She lashes out at her new friends, sometimes dangerously, and tries to attack them when she has mental breaks that she can't control.

An article from the Dana Foundation on brain trauma includes the observation that "humans process vast amounts of information. We can function only by being strategically selective in our awareness. To do otherwise would be like having every stored file in a computer open at once, or all the contents of one's office file cabinets spread out on the desk at the same time."[xcii] In River's case, she is opening *everyone's* file cabinets at once with no choice in the matter. She doesn't have control over what she feels or hears, which increases her mental instability.

COGNITIVE PROCESSING THERAPY

To help River feel safe in the present moment and deal with her trauma, Dr. Scarlet recommends a technique that other heroes throughout the book have found useful: *cognitive processing therapy*. "CPT allows individuals to process their trauma in a safe way, as well as to learn to distinguish true danger from perceived danger, the latter of which can arise when a trauma survivor gets triggered or reminded of their traumatic experience," she explains. Something like CPT means that River would go through the process of evaluating and changing her upsetting thoughts so that there are less moments when she might be triggered unknowingly—for example, she may blame herself for the fact that her brother gave up his successful medical career to rescue her, or she may blame herself for hurting her friends when she couldn't control her reactions. Using CPT, however, River would be able to assess whether or not these facts she believes about herself really are true . . . and come to the realization on her own that she is not responsible for all of her trauma.

LEARNING FROM A HERO

River's brother Simon Tam administers semiregular medication treatments to help her, giving us another reminder that we shouldn't be afraid or ashamed of taking medication as a way to help us through trauma. Being surrounded by the Firefly crew and having spent time with friendly and caring company also allows River to begin to overcome her instability.

"I think when you talk about the social support and the family that surrounds River, *this* is giving her that sense of belonging," says Dr. Letamendi. "*This* is giving her that sense of meaning and purpose. And following severe trauma, a lot of times throughout that recovery phase, there's a recalibration of sense of self and sense of the world. *Why do I matter? Why should I continue? What is my purpose moving forward? I've been objectified, I've been mutilated, I've been dehumanized, and so how do I gain a sense of humanity back? What is my purpose?* And the *Firefly* crew gives her that sense of belonging. They give her that sense of participation as a member of their family, and that is the work that is done naturally through their close bonds of their relationship."

River never knew normalcy because she was taken from her home at an early age and forced to give up any semblance of her old life, adopting what the Academy felt was a "correct" way to live. But because she surrounds herself with good people, she's reminded that she *does* have a place in this world, and that it's okay to laugh—that it's okay to make mistakes and, sometimes, that it's even okay to be vulnerable.

ALONE IN DYSTOPIA

Gender inequality exists in fictional worlds and video games as much as it does in the real world. According to an article from *ScienceDaily*, "recent research suggests that young girls are more sensitive to social stress than boys. This could mean that social networks are more important for females in general, and that young females . . . may be more sensitive toward social isolation than males."[xciii]

Until the Naughty Dog® video game *The Last of Us*, which debuted in 2013, the world had been hard-pressed to find a female protagonist in the gaming sphere who was both complex and powerful. A teen survivor of a fungal pandemic living in a post-apocalyptic United States, Ellie has been lauded for her self-sufficient personality, her smarts, and her emotional strength. But it's not only Ellie's emotional traits that make her complex: it's the raw and stark depiction of her mental health and her journey toward overcoming her demons.

MONOPHOBIA

Despite only being a teenager, because she grew up alone, Ellie adapts quickly to a self-sufficient life that builds on her already tough and brash attitude. When she arrives at her quarantine zone, she declares she can take care of herself. When she meets Riley Abel, the girl who will become her best friend, she brushes off words of advice on how to survive in her new home. Ellie tends to "supervise" adults by inserting herself into their conversations or taking "justice" into her own hands, whether that's through violence or through a verbal exchange.

Even though Ellie's confidence comes from being able to take care of herself, her mental health is another story. In a few different instances in the game, such as a cut scene with protagonist Joel when she lashes out at him for leaving unexpectedly and when she tells another survivor she's scared of losing people she cares about, it's heavily implied that Ellie suffers from *monophobia*, also known as *autophobia*, which is defined as a morbid dread of being alone. A specific phobia of isolation, individuals suffering from monophobia don't need to be alone physically—they're usually triggered by the thought of spending time alone or the thought of being abandoned.[xciv] In Ellie's case, her monophobia comes directly from her physical isolation; she's never known life outside of a zombie apocalypse. Growing up in an orphanage in an oppressive military quarantine zone in Boston, Ellie is devoid of any real family and is afforded little knowledge about the outside world. Ellie's monophobia causes her to live in fear that she will lose the people she cares about, like Joel, who becomes a partner of sorts during their journey together. This feeling is exacerbated by the fact that, throughout the game, she loses both her best friend and her guardian. Her monophobia also feeds on her prickly nature, as she becomes even more withdrawn and distrusting, not knowing how to form relationships with other people due to being isolated for so long.

SURVIVOR'S GUILT

Something happens: you feel responsible. Something doesn't happen: you still feel responsible, because survivor's guilt is an endless loop of feelings that range from irrational to reasonable. "Subjective guilt, associated with this sense of responsibility, is thought to be irrational because one feels guilty despite the fact that he knows he has done nothing wrong," explains a *New York Times* article. "Objective or rational guilt, by contrast—guilt that is 'fitting' to one's actions—accurately tracks real wrongdoing or culpability: guilt is appropriate because one acted to deliberately harm someone, or could have prevented harm and did not."[xcv]

When Ellie and Riley are attacked and infected with the fungal parasite while on the run together, Riley proposes two options: commit suicide, or live out the rest of their time together. Choosing the latter, Riley and Ellie both await their fate—but in the end, it's only Riley who dies, as Ellie turns out to be immune to the infection. Ellie is wrecked with survivor's guilt over the fact that fate has chosen to keep her alive, and this is part of the reason she decides to allow herself to be used to find a cure for the pandemic that has ravaged the United States. She feels that that her sacrifice, even if it ends in death, would be beneficial to others.

When Ellie accepts this path, she's scared about what could happen. But because of her survivor's guilt, she feels like this is the only way she can be wanted or needed in the world—by doing something that would make every death she witnessed meaningful.

Ellie's survivor's guilt doesn't end with Riley. She loses Tess, Joel's smuggling friend and her guardian, and blames herself for Tess's death because she knows Tess sacrificed herself thinking Ellie was most important as the "cure for mankind." When Ellie meets another group of survivors in the form of two brothers, Sam and Henry, she's heartened to find people who share her worldview—kids who are around the same age and who have grown up on the same dystopian planet. When Sam becomes infected, he tries to subtly tell Ellie because he doesn't want to hurt her, but he doesn't actually alert her to the fact he's going to die. The suddenness of his death affects her heavily.

LEARNING FROM A HERO

According to an article from the Sylvia Brafman Mental Health Center, "While survivors of disasters or traumatic events tend to cope differently, many find that . . . talking about their feelings with a friend, loved one, or counselor helps. Taking time to mourn the loss of those who perished in the event can be difficult but can be a big step in the coping process, too."[xcvi]

Ellie shows us that by being responsible and confident, you can face your own fears. We may not live in a zombie apocalypse, but Ellie reminds us that we do need to depend on some kind of relationship or found family to get through difficult times. Joel tells Ellie that the secret to survival is to find something to keep fighting for—for them, it's their family and their bond they don't want to lose, because they have already lost so much between them.

In a *New York Times* op-ed titled "Game Theory: The Last of Us, Revisited," Alexandria Neonakis, a member of the team that created *The Last of Us*, wrote of Ellie, "She's powerful the whole time, and it had nothing to do with wielding a gun or physical ability. In an industry that more often than not represents women as either a damsel in distress or a male character in a female body, this was a triumph in storytelling and representation. Ellie is an entirely playable character. It was not by coincidence that the moments you play as her are the most impactful in the game."[xcvii]

ALONE IN THE CASTLE

A study from UCLA suggests that a loving parental figure can influence a child's health and lifespan, and that "the negative impact of childhood abuse or lack of parental affection can take a mental and physical toll [that] can also last a lifetime. Childhood neglect increases adult risk for morbidity and mortality."[xcviii]

Cersei Lannister is a character who seems to have no gray area: you either love her for being a power-hungry queen who puts herself first at the expense of others, or you hate her for the same reason. In both George R. R. Martin's *Game of Thrones* books and in the popular HBO® television show, Cersei's actions are clear: this is a girl who was forced to live a certain way of life, but now that she is able to hold power in her hands, she is letting nothing hold her back. Given Cersei's obsession (to an incestuous degree) with her twin Jaime, it's easy to assume that her motivations stem from a love for her brother. While that's true, Ceresi's motivations also come from within herself, which fits with the upbringing she experienced—a childhood contributed to her current state of mental health.

A YOUNG QUEEN

Even though Cersei is an adult, her emotional maturity is that of a wayward teenager—someone who has never experienced any real parenting. According to the UCLA study, "Findings suggest that parental warmth and affection protect one against the harmful effects of toxic childhood stress."[xcix] Cersei's childish nature, despite her calm and regal control, is something that was built into her over time, and it's reflected in how poor of a mother she is to her own children. She's unable to provide them with their own moral compasses and treats them as extensions of herself as opposed to caring for their well-being, such as when she uses them as pawns in her play for taking the throne of Westeros.

"People like Cersei Lannister, who experienced parental loss at an early age while being ignored by the surviving parent, may sometimes engage in maladaptive and even violent behaviors," Dr. Scarlet explains. Born in a time when men governed and women were meant to sit on the sidelines, Cersei was raised both in privilege and in isolation: her mother died when she was four years old, leaving Cersei in the care of her father, Tywin, who spent most of his time away from the family since he was serving the king. Instead of caring or attentive parents, Cersei's upbringing came from servants.

ARRANGED MARRIAGE

Not only did Cersei not get a choice about how she grew up, she did not get a choice about who she married. And when she finally tried to make a life for herself, her father forced her into a relationship in a move that was entirely political. According to *Psychology Today*, "A common rationale for arranged marriages is that young people are too immature and impulsive to make a wise choice, and experienced elders are likely to do better."[c] Although Cersei was nineteen and technically of legal age when she was forced into marrying Robert Baratheon, she was still young and inexperienced in navigating the world, and her mental state was still that of a child. While the *Game of Thrones* series takes place in a fictional, medieval setting entirely different from our modern way of life, the traditions portrayed in the show aren't too far removed from real-life situations. Researchers have found that "girls under eighteen who get married are more likely to experience mental health problems, including depression, anxiety, and bipolar disorders. They are also more likely to become dependent on alcohol, drugs, and nicotine."[ci] Throughout *Game of Thrones*, especially as the series progresses and battles and personal issues become more intense, we see Cersei relying on alcohol more and more when she's alone. And although we don't see enough of her drinking to classify this habit as alcoholism, it's fair to assume that her stressful upbringing has led to unhealthy habits.

ISOLATION AND BLAME

Blame is a part of a self-defense mechanism called *rationalization*, something that people who are isolated or depressed usually use to mask their pain. When you rationalize something, you try to explain it by attributing the blame you don't want to take responsibility for to someone or something else. Dr. Whitbourne writes in *Psychology Today* that "people often use rationalization to shore up their insecurities or remorse after doing something they regret, such as an 'oops' moment. It's easier to blame someone else than to take the heat yourself, particularly if you would otherwise feel shame or embarrassment."[cii]

The restraints placed on Cersei because she is a woman are far-reaching; she's not only jealous of the freedom men have to rule and make decisions, but her lineage in particular has a strict policy when it comes to women's privileges. Cersei isn't taught skills of negotiation like her father and brothers are, and her isolation makes it easy to blame others for her shortcomings. "Individuals with histories similar to Cersei's may perceive disagreements as rejection and disloyalty, viewing these as potential threats," says Dr. Scarlet. "When an individual with a history like Cersei's feels threatened, they might react in an impulsive and destructive way rather than attempt to compromise."

Much of Cersei's life is ruled by the blame she places on others instead of herself. She places her son on the throne and then blames her younger brother Tyrion for his death—an action that was brought on by events *she* put into motion. She blames her father for forcing her into an unhappy marriage, even though she *did* genuinely love her husband at the beginning of their relationship.

LEARNING FROM A HERO

Although Cersei is fiercely independent and wouldn't seek anyone's help willingly, she's proven to be most vulnerable when she's around others who understand her plight as both a woman and as a mother. If Cersei was willing to go into therapy, she might learn how to accept some of the blame she always places on others, allowing her to take responsibility for her own actions. By establishing trust, Cersei would be able to realize she isn't as alone as she thinks she is. That kind of social acceptance would not only help her accept her mistakes but allow her to see that she's not the terrible person everyone believes she is—helping her realize that there are people out there who know and believe she can be the strong-willed queen she was always meant to be.

ALONE IN SOCIETY

Whether we realize it or not, we all need human connection—not just to enrich our lives, but to keep our mental health intact. "Humans are hardwired to interact with others, especially during times of stress," says Frank McAndrew, PhD, in an article for *Psychology Today*. "When we go through a trying ordeal alone, a lack of emotional support and friendship can increase our anxiety and hinder our coping ability."[ciii]

Rogue is an X-Men mutant whose powers include the ability to drain a living person's essence upon skin-to-skin contact, meaning she can absorb someone's physical skills, memories, and personality traits. And if Rogue lets herself touch someone for too long, such as in an act of intimacy, her touch can prove fatal. Because of the nature of her powers, Rogue spends most of her life isolated and shying away from human interaction, fearful of hurting people she loves. Rogue may not be the superhero who immediately comes to mind when we think of inspiration and strength—but we should think of her, because the strength with which Rogue overcame her isolation *is* something to be inspired by.

SOCIAL ISOLATION

Social isolation differs from loneliness, as loneliness is usually defined as a temporary lack of contact with others. Social isolation is an almost complete lack of contact between individuals and society. According to a 2016 *New York Times* article, "social isolation is a growing epidemic—one that's increasingly recognized as having dire physical, mental and emotional consequences. Since the 1980s, the percentage of American adults who say they're lonely has doubled from 20 percent to 40 percent." The long-term effects, the study notes, start early, as "socially isolated children have significantly poorer health twenty years later."[civ]

Rogue's first experience with her powers is one that most young girls would count as their most significant moment: her first kiss. Unaware of how her powers work, the act of intimacy between her and her childhood crush proves nearly fatal when her crush ends up in a permanent coma, an experience that traumatizes Rogue for most of her life and leads her to believe that her powers are more of a curse than a gift. She covers herself in skin-concealing clothing and leaves her home soon after the incident to live in isolation, fearing that she can't come into contact with or get close to anyone because she'll hurt them. "New research suggests that loneliness is not necessarily the result of poor social skills or lack of social support, but can be caused in part by unusual sensitivity to social cues," the *New York Times* article continues. "Lonely people are more likely to perceive ambiguous social cues negatively, and enter a self-preservation mindset—worsening the problem."[cv]

Although barely a teenager, Rogue begins isolating herself early, and this loneliness becomes a way of life. "We learn so much about ourselves because of the people around us, and being around them shapes us. Not only do our parents play a large role in our development, but also our siblings and peers," says Dr. Saborsky. "Because Rogue was isolated for such a large portion of her life, there is a possibility that she would be a totally different person if she had not been isolated. There is still debate on whether nature or nurture leads us to be the people we are. As an individual with a background in developmental psychology, it is my belief that her brain would be very different from someone who is not isolated. Her isolation would most likely impact her social skills with others, the way she copes with situations and understands adversity, and could even cause her difficulty when it comes to relating to peers."

MENTAL BLOCKS

Social isolation aside, Rogue's greatest flaw has always been her inability to control her powers. Like Storm, she was never taught how to understand and control the gifts she was given. Most of Rogue's "learning experiences" came from using her powers and seeing the consequences of what she could and couldn't do to people. Her real guidance eventually comes from Professor Xavier, the founder and leader of the X-Men, in the comic *X-Men: Legacy* #224, when he teaches her how to control her mind.[cvi]

Research has shown that long-term social isolation not only has mental health effects—it also changes the brain. "Chronic social isolation actually affects the brain's chemistry and leads to negative behavioral changes,"[cvii] says a 2018 study published in the journal *Cell*. Because Rogue isolated herself from the world for so long, she had built up a mental block that was hindering her ability to understand

and control the powers she always thought were doomed to segregate her. With Professor X's help, Rogue realizes that what's really keeping her from controlling her powers properly is her own mind—the insecurities and doubts that have built up from years of isolating herself, feeling guilty for hurting others, and being afraid to get close to people. Once Rogue realizes what her mental blocks are, she is able to work toward overcoming them, which allows her to slowly reemerge into society, develop relationships, and find friends again. "We are social creatures and need others to grow and learn. The idea that it takes a village to help a child grow is no lie," says Dr. Saborsky. "Having others around us at times is what makes us, us."

LEARNING FROM A HERO

Professor X is known for being one of the most important guardians of the X-Men, and he acts as an important person in Rogue's life; he is, in essence, her therapist. Xavier gives Rogue someone to talk to who she can trust and not worry about hurting, which helps Rogue learn how to feel comfortable with human interaction.

Therapy is a powerful and important option that we can pursue when we are feeling alone, as therapists can help us break through what we might not be able to on our own. Even though Professor X was a friend, he was removed enough from Rogue's situation that she didn't feel like he would judge her for her past. Because of that, Rogue started to heal and was finally able to realize she didn't have to be alone—she could control her own powers and her own life.

ALONE IN THE WORLD

As Supergirl shows, when we are saddled with responsibility, it can be overwhelming. It can also be mentally exhausting and cause us to second-guess our mental health. "Existential therapists believe that it is neither genes nor environment . . . that determines our behavior, but *how we choose to respond* to our genes and environment," says PhD lecturer Mikhail Lyubansky in an essay published in *The Psychology of Joss Whedon: An Unauthorized Exploration of Buffy, Angel, and Firefly.*[cviii] "According to existential tenets, people are often afraid of freedom (to choose) because with freedom to choose comes the possibility of choosing poorly. With freedom, in other words, comes responsibility."

Ask anyone with an inkling of pop culture knowledge, and you'll find that Buffy Summers is widely heralded as one of the most formidable and important females in pop culture. Is it because she slays vampires and saves the world while also doing her homework? Definitely. Is it also because she shows us how to overcome the isolation of intense responsibility, while still allowing us to see her vulnerability and mental health issues? Absolutely.

A TEENAGE BURDEN

On the surface, Buffy is the picture-perfect depiction of a perky, blond, California teen undergoing all the trials and tribulations of high school. But what Buffy deals with, often in isolation, is something no one could ever understand. Known as a "Slayer," Buffy represents the chosen person—one per generation—whose fate is tasked with saving the world from monsters, zombies, and otherworldly horrors. Loneliness and isolation are very much a part of a Slayer's legacy, and this particular plight is Buffy's alone.

After receiving her powers at fifteen years old, Buffy's Slayer duties essentially become a full-time job. She gives up parties, a social life, her friends, and relationships in order to spend her nights and weekends patrolling the streets of Sunnydale, keeping the city from harm. Because Buffy is a Slayer, she feels fundamentally different from her friends. She has duties she can't just ignore if she's feeling off for a night, and like B'Elanna and Jennifer Walters, Buffy is constantly struggling with two sides of herself: the Slayer side, aka the world's protector, and the "Buffy" side, aka the daughter, sister, and friend. Buffy's Slayer side often tells her to stay in isolation and fight alone, while her "Buffy" side encourages her to open up to her friends and ask for help.

"Adolescence is hard enough for most people. However, having the pressure to keep the world safe from vampires can make it far more challenging," says Dr. Scarlet. "Many teenagers already feel misunderstood, isolated, and overwhelmed by balancing school and social life. Buffy, however, also has to miss out on important social events due to training, continuously put her life in danger, have her heart broken, and have to lie to her mother and teachers."

ISOLATION AND DEATH

At the end of the fourth season of *Buffy the Vampire Slayer*, Buffy has a dream where she confronts the very first Slayer, who drives home the fact that Buffy's role as the "Chosen One" means that she will forever be isolated. By living in the shadow of death, she will always be surrounded by tragedy and will always worry about dying without being able to live a normal life. There is no instance where Buffy feels more isolated than when her friends resurrect her, five months after she sacrifices her life to save her sister.[cix] Assuming that Buffy would want to be brought back to life, her friends make the choice to perform a resurrection ritual. Their goodwill backfires, however, as it turns out that Buffy was actually happier in her afterlife than she had been in the real world.

After her death and resurrection, Buffy's social isolation becomes her obstacle. She resents her friends for bringing her back and withdraws from them, not wanting them to know how unhappy she is. She feels like she has no place in a world she hates, one that is full of anger and stress and violence, and begins having recurring nightmares indicative of PTSD. She was brought back to be around people who love her, but she is suddenly more alone than ever. "When Buffy returned from the dead, she was taken from a peaceful, meditative place and returned to a world that was much harsher than what she experienced at rest," says Dr. Saborsky. "When she came back, that solace was taken from her. It's a big jolt. In real life, I might look at her return as similar to going back to work or being around other people 'normally' after a major death in your family or with a friend. It's really difficult for patients who are dealing with trauma to be around people who are happy and haven't experienced this strange, awful thing. It takes a lot of new tools and readjustment to get back to a place where you can identify with people who haven't gone through this major thing you've gone through."

A SLAYER'S RESPONSIBILITY

Buffy's biggest test is not slaying vampires; it's learning how to accept responsibility. "Even though none of us can know for certain how our actions will impact the world around us, we still have to wish and decide and then take responsibility for those decisions," says Lyubansky.[cx] Buffy knows that every choice she makes, whether it's a vampire kill or a decision to hide parts of her life from her friends and family, can have a consequence. As the series progresses, Buffy eventually confides in her mentor that she's thinking of letting herself off the hook of responsibility for awhile.

THE SCOOBY GANG: the pop culture reference to Buffy's group of high school friends, who help her in her Slayer duties throughout the series

Until Buffy meets her friends (the **"Scooby Gang"**), she doesn't tell anyone else what she does or attempt to invite them into her dangerous life. Buffy remains largely alone throughout her journey, carrying the responsibility of the world on her shoulders—a responsibility she never asked for and can't get rid of. "When people, especially teenagers, have the pressure of being responsible for other people's lives, they may feel as if no one else can understand or help them," says Dr. Scarlet. "Losing loved ones, experiencing trauma, and undergoing significant life changes, as Buffy does throughout the series, can also have that effect."

LEARNING FROM A HERO

Perhaps the most valuable self-help lesson Buffy can teach us is that we really are better when we don't have to fight our literal and figurative monsters alone. When Buffy first returns from the dead, she's too overwhelmed to seek out any kind of help. Throughout different instances in Buffy's life, she pushes her friends away whenever life gets hard—when she has too many responsibilities, when she's grieving, when she feels unable to help people she loves, when she's angry. Gradually, however, she finds that being honest with her found family allows her to open up in other ways. Reengaging with her friends and admitting what she's going through also allows Buffy to find her new purpose, which isn't slaying or protecting the world. It's spending time with and protecting the important people in her life: her friends, her family, and her sister. Buffy's mental health struggles are based on who she is—she is the Slayer, but she is also simply a human girl. As she tells us, "the hardest thing in this world . . . is to live in it. Be brave. Live."[cxi]

No matter what obstacles we are facing and no matter how hopeless life may seem, we can all be brave.

PRACTICING SELF-CARE:
Lessons from Buffy Summers

We may not be Slayers who have to stake vampires and destroy evil beings like Buffy Summers, but we *are* Slayers when it comes to the demons and monsters of our own mental health. Here's what Buffy can teach us when it comes to taking care of ourselves and conquering our own fears.

1. **Make yourself responsible for your own mental health.** Buffy learns the hard way that by taking care of everyone else, she's not taking care of herself. Giving herself the emotional space and vulnerability to grieve, breathe, cry, or show her emotions helps her grow and become a better Slayer. By letting your guard down and putting yourself first, you can improve your mindset and create a healthier mental space for yourself.

2. **Find a chosen family you can trust.** There's no doubt about it: Buffy suffers more when she tries to carry her burdens herself and is most powerful when she lets her friends help her. You may have blood family, but it's important to surround yourself with a chosen second family that believes in you, trusts you, and will help pick you up when you fall.

3. **Try to accept what hurts, even if you want to run from it.** Buffy wants to shut her friends and the world out when she comes back from the dead, when her mother dies, and when her boyfriend breaks up with her. But by accepting these bad moments and letting them shape her, she is able to live her life more fully and understand the world around her with more clarity, especially when it comes to helping and saving people. Letting trusted friends or family into your life during hard times not only helps you heal, it can make you stronger.

SUMALEE MONTANO[cxii]

@SUMALEEDOTCOM

Sumalee Montano is an actress who has appeared in television shows like *Veep, Scandal, Nashville, This Is Us,* and *The West Wing.* As a voice actor, she can be heard in national commercials as well as on animated programs such as *Voltron, Marvel's Guardians of the Galaxy,* and *Transformers: Prime,* and she can be seen on *Critical Role* and in the video game *Destiny 2.*

Q: **Who is the female character that you identify with most when it comes to personal struggles, and why?**

A: I'd say the daughters in *The Joy Luck Club* by Amy Tan. I can't pick just one. There's something in each of the daughters' stories—about finding their voices and forging their identities as Asian American women—that I really relate with. I also see my relationship with my mother reflected in their stories, too. The mother-daughter relationship is so special, so fraught, so beautiful, and powerful. Even years after reading this book, I still find myself moved by the characters' mother-daughter stories.

Q: Why do you think we, as artists/individuals, identify so much with characters who have undergone mental health struggles, even though we know they're fictional?

A: Actors empathize by nature. I think part of the reason we're drawn to characters undergoing mental health struggles is because of the invisibility of the struggle. You can't necessarily look at someone and know they're dealing with mental health issues. It's completely different than seeing someone struggling with, say, a broken leg. We want to understand and empathize with the hidden struggle.

Also, I think most people know someone who has struggled with mental health issues. We're drawn to these characters because we want to empathize with the people in our own lives who face similar challenges.

Q: What have the female characters you've worked on in your creative endeavors taught you when it comes to overcoming your own obstacles?

A: Embrace the mistakes you're going to make along the way. They're inevitable. No one's perfect, so be gentle with yourself.

I used to abhor making mistakes. Subconsciously I strove to be a perfect daughter, the perfect actor, friend, etc. And of course, I was constantly letting myself down, because perfect is impossible. Then after my mom died, I finally realized that she never would have wanted a "perfect daughter" in me. I thought she did. But she would have thought that was boring! It was such a wonderful realization for me. Nowadays, I never aim for

100 percent. It's the flaws that make me, the characters I play, and the journey more interesting.

Also, don't think you have to overcome obstacles on your own. I'm thinking specifically of the characters Arcee, Katana, and Nila (from *Critical Role*). Accepting help and support from others is a necessary part of overcoming challenges.

Q: **What advice can you give to people who might be struggling to find their own light in a dark place?**

A: After my mom died, which was the hardest thing I've gone through, I found that developing my spirituality helped a lot. It may sound cliché, but it helped pull me through my darkest times.

A lot of people would suggest seeking professional help, and I agree with that, too. If you aren't able to, try telling a friend who you think might seek help for you or with you. When I was dealing with the sudden death of my youngest cousin, I couldn't get myself to ask for professional help. I'd never done that before. I ended up telling a friend what I was dealing with. They came over to my apartment, listened, and literally wouldn't let me leave until we made some calls together and I had made an appointment with a therapist. It was what I needed at that time—the therapy and a friend who made me pick up the phone and call. It was a lifesaver.

CONCLUSION

t's easy to believe that we're alone—that we don't need anyone else to help us. But, like Black Widow says in Marvel's *Avengers: Infinity War,* when she and Wakandan general Okoye come to the aid of Scarlet Witch during the heat of the final battle: "She's not alone." And neither are we. With the help of our friends, our family, individuals who have gone through similar hardships, and outside help, we can find kinship. With the help of fictional women who show us how to overcome our struggles, we can be brave. By leaning on the doctors, the FBI agents, the spies, the mutants, the witches, the druids, the superheroes, and the aliens, we can find acceptance, we can be strong, and we can persevere.

So, like Buffy asks a future generation of Slayers who have gathered to help her save the world, I now ask you: "Make your choice. Are you ready to be strong?"[cxiii]

ABOUT THE EXPERTS

Dr. Andrea Letamendi holds a PhD in clinical psychology and regularly brings attention to the psychological themes found in pop culture characters, movies, and science fiction. In addition to being published by organizations such as *The Atlantic* and the *American Psychological Association*, Dr. Letamendi speaks on panels and seminars at universities, mental health agencies, and pop culture events. She also cohosts a monthly *Star Wars*–themed podcast called *Lattes with Leia* and has presented a TED Talk on merging her love of superheroes with her professional work. Dr. Letamendi currently works as an associate director of Mental Health Training, Intervention, and Response for the Office of Residential Life at UCLA.

Dr. Janina Scarlet is a licensed clinical psychologist, author, and full-time geek. She came to the US as a refugee and went on to develop Superhero Therapy to help patients with anxiety, depression, trauma, and chronic pain disorders, by using fictional characters and geek culture such as *Harry Potter*, *Doctor Who*, *Batman*, *Star Wars*, *Lord of the Rings*, and others in order to help her patients. Dr. Scarlet has coauthored and contributed to numerous books about psychology and pop culture and frequently speaks on panels that focus on mental health.

Dr. Amy Saborsky is a licensed psychologist focused on the assessment and treatment of children and adolescents in a private practice setting. She earned her bachelor of science degree in psychology from DeSales University and her master's degree at La Salle University, where she also completed her PsyD in clinical psychology with a focus on child and adolescent psychology. Dr. Saborsky has had multiple experiences in the field of clinical and research psychology with both children and adults. She currently holds an adjunct role at DeSales and is the owner and director of her own practice, the Lehigh Valley Center for Child and Family Development.

THANK YOU

I t's easy to say or think "I want to write a book" but it's harder to make that happen—and trust me when I say that this book would not have happened without the help, support, and guidance of many people.

Thank you to Maria Vicente for not only being my rockstar agent, but for believing in me and working so hard to make my dream come true. It's because of Maria that *Geek Girls Don't Cry* found a home at Sterling and with my fantastic editor, Kate Zimmermann. Thank you, Kate, for your patience and wisdom; your ideas, vision, and guidance have been a gift. Thank you to my tireless copyeditor Kayla Overbey, whose smart suggestions lifted this book to another (dare I say better) level. Thank you to Paulina Ganucheau for producing the most gorgeous cover that made me cry the first time I saw it in my inbox. And a huge grateful thank you to the entire team at Sterling, particularly publicist extraordinaire Blanca Oliviery who showed a first-time author the publicity ropes, and wizard designers Shannon Nicole Plunkett and David Ter-Avanesyan who helped put together these beautiful pages. I feel so lucky to have worked with such a wonderful team!

Choosing who will write a foreword for your very first book is not a decision any author takes lightly, but I was lucky enough to know exactly whose voice I wanted to represent my writing. I am even luckier that she wrote something so perfect, filled with the same honesty and strength that she consistently shows the world. Thank you, Marisha— your drive, courage, and talent make me proud to be a part of your life.

This book is filled with women who are not only inspirational in their own right, but also fierce and powerful in knowledge. *Geek Girls Don't Cry* would not be what it is without my talented contributors, each of whom was unfailingly kind and allowed me to borrow their insight and time. Thank you Andrea Letamendi, Janina Scarlet, Amy Saborsky, and Robyn Warren—I am so thrilled that you came on this journey with me! Thank you Margie Stohl, Kelly Sue DeConnick, Catrina Dennis, Sam Maggs, and Sumalee Montano—I am so honored to have the pleasure of sharing your stories with the world.

Thank you to my own tribe of geek girls who definitely don't cry but definitely *do* inspire me on a daily basis: Sarah, Katie, Kait, Carrie, Heather, Leslie, Cate, and Eileen.

There is no art without inspiration, and I would be remiss if I didn't say thank you to the women behind these fictional characters, particularly the ones who have had such a hand in shaping my life: Gillian Anderson, Scarlett Johansson, Elizabeth Mitchell, and Emma Watson.

Thank you to East One Coffee Roasters in Brooklyn for providing me with both wine *and* caffeine, and for letting me commandeer a table near an outlet for hours on end while I wrote and edited this manuscript.

Thank you to my husband Brendan for putting up with me throughout this publishing journey and for supporting me so deeply. Thank you to my parents, Elyssa and David, for never letting me run from my dreams no matter the cost. Thank you to my sister, Rebecca, for showing me what it means to have a true sidekick of unconditional love.

And thank you to *you*, reader, for being a part of this manifesto of geek empowerment. Whoever you saw yourself in and whatever struggles you are facing, I hope that you were able to find a little bit of light within these pages.

ABOUT THE AUTHOR

ANDREA TOWERS has a BA in English and communications from The George Washington University and an MS in journalism from Northwestern University. A love of going to the movies regularly, reading at the table during dinner, and making sure she taped every single episode of *The X-Files* led her to a career in the entertainment industry, where she has worked for over a decade. Andrea has written about comics and pop culture as an assistant editor and writer at *Entertainment Weekly* and has worked professionally in the comics industry in public relations for Marvel Entertainment. She has also contributed writing on pop culture to a number of publications both in print and online.

Andrea lives in New York City with her husband. She owns three different coffee makers and will forever hold the opinion that *The Lord of the Rings* movies are a cinematic masterpiece. You can visit her at andrea-towers.com.

 @_atowers

 @_andreatowers

NOTES

i   Andrea Letamendi (clinical psychologist) in discussion with the author, August 2018.

ii   "PTSD: National Center For PTSD," US Department of Veterans Affairs, last updated September 24, 2018, https://www.ptsd.va.gov/understand/common/common_adults.asp

iii   Michael Schreiner, "Repetition Compulsion," Evolution Counseling, Oct. 4, 2017, https://evolutioncounseling.com/repetition-compulsion/.

iv   Ibid.

v   *Avengers: Age of Ultron*, directed by Joss Whedon (2015; Hollywood, CA: Marvel Studios, Paramount Pictures), Film.

vi   Claire Cain Miller, "The Motherhood Penalty vs. the Fatherhood Bonus," *The New York Times*, Sep. 6, 2014, https://www.nytimes.com/2014/09/07/upshot/a-child-helps-your-career-if-youre-a-man.html.

vii   "Employment Characteristics of Families Summary," US Bureau of Labor Statistics, last modified Apr. 19, 2018, https://www.bls.gov/news.release/famee.nr0.htm.

viii   "PTSD: National Center For PTSD," US Department of Veterans Affairs, last updated September 24, 2018, https://www.ptsd.va.gov/understand/common/common_women.asp

ix   Ruth Eveleth, "Women Are the Invisible Victims of PTSD," Motherboard, May 5, 2016, https://motherboard.vice.com/en_us/article/ezpvwn/ptsd-isnt-just-for-soldiers.

x   Susanne Babbel, "Domestic Violence: Power Struggle With Lasting Consequences," *Psychology Today*, May 27, 2011, https://www.psychologytoday.com/us/blog/somatic-psychology/201105/domestic-violence-power-struggle-lasting-consequences.

xi *The Avengers*, directed by Joss Whedon (2012; Hollywood, CA: Marvel Studios, Paramount Pictures), Film.

xii Stan Lee and N. Korok, *Tales of Suspense* Vol. 1, #52, New York, NY: Marvel Comics, 1964.

xiii Adam Goldman, "Where Are Women in F.B.I.'s Top Ranks?" *The New York Times*, Oct. 22, 2016, https://www.nytimes.com/2016/10/23/us/fbi-women.html.

xiv Ellen Kirschman, "Cops and PTSD," *Psychology Today*, Jun. 26, 2017, https://www.psychologytoday.com/us/blog/cop-doc/201706/cops-and-ptsd-0.

xv Tara A. Hartley, Khachatur Sarkisian, John M. Violanti, Michael E. Andrew, Cecil M. Burchfiel, "PTSD Symptoms Among Police Officers: Associations with Frequency, Recency, and Types of Traumatic Events." *International Journal of Emergency Mental Health and Human Resilience* 15, no. 4 (2013): 241–253, https://www.ncbi.nlm.nih.gov/pmc/articles/PMC4734407/.

xvi Alane Lim, "What Is Survivor's Guilt? Definition and Examples," ThoughtCo., Aug. 13, 2018, https://www.thoughtco.com/survivors-guilt-definition-examples-4173110.

xvii 21st Century Fox, Geena Davis Institute on Gender in Media, and J. Walter Thompson Intelligence, "The 'Scully Effect': I Want to Believe . . . in STEM," 21CF Social Impact, accessed Nov. 18, 2018, https://impact.21cf.com/wp-content/uploads/sites/2/2018/03/ScullyEffectReport_21CF_1-1.pdf.

xviii National Research Council and Institute of Medicine of the National Academies, "Depression in Parents, Parenting, and Children," 2009, *National Academies Press*, doi: 10.17226/12565, https://www.nap.edu/read/12565/chapter/1#ii.

xix "PTSD: National Center For PTSD," US Department of Veteran Affairs, last updated Aug. 13, 2015, https://www.ptsd.va.gov/public/ptsd-overview/women/traumatic-stress-female-vets.asp.

xx *Xena: Warrior Princess*, season 1, episode 1, "Sins of the Past," directed by Doug Lefler, aired Sept. 4, 1995, on FOX.

xxi Saul McLeod, "Maslow's Hierarchy of Needs," *Simply Psychology*, May 2018, https://www.simplypsychology.org/maslow.html.

xxii   Ibid.

xxiii   Davey, Graham. 1997. *Phobias: a Handbook of Theory, Research, and Treatment.* Chichester: Wiley.

xxiv   Janina Scarlet (clinical psychologist) in discussion with the author, July 2018.

xxv   Chris Claremont, *X-Men* Vol. 1, #102, New York, NY: Marvel Comics, 1976.

xxvi   Chris Claremont, *Uncanny X-Men* Vol. 1, #147, New York, NY: Marvel Comics, 1981.

xxvii   Jason Aaron, *Wolverine and the X-Men* Vol. 1, #24, New York, NY: Marvel Comics, 2013.

xxviii   Margaret Stohl (author) in discussion with the author, August 2017.

xxix   James Gillies and Robert A. Neimeyer, "Loss, Grief, and the Search for Significance: Toward a Model of Meaning Reconstruction in Bereavement," *Journal of Constructivist Psychology* 19, no. 1: 31–65 (2006), DOI: 10.1080/10720530500311182.

xxx   Amy Saborsky (clinical psychologist) in discussion with the author, August 2018.

xxxi   "Overview," Center for Complicated Grief at Columbia School of Social Work, 2017, https://complicatedgrief.columbia.edu/professionals/ complicated-grief-professionals/overview/.

xxxii   Deborah Khoshaba, "About Complicated Bereavement Disorder," *Psychology Today*, Sept. 28, 2013, https://www.psychologytoday.com/us/ blog/get-hardy/201309/about-complicated-bereavement-disorder-0.

xxxiii   Institute of Medicine Committee for the Study of Health Consequences of the Stress of Bereavement, "Bereavement During Childhood and Adolescence," in *Bereavement: Reactions, Consequences, and Care*, eds. Frederic Solomon, Marian Osterweis, and Morris Green (National Academies Press: Washington, DC, 1984), 99–143,https://www.ncbi.nlm. nih.gov/books/NBK217849/.

xxxiv   Ralph Ryback, "The Ways We Grieve," *Psychology Today*, Feb. 27, 2017, https://www.psychologytoday.com/us/blog/the-truisms-wellness/201702/ the-ways-we-grieve.

xxxv   Ibid.

xxxvi Frédérique Autin and Jean-Claude Croizet, "Improving Working Memory Efficiency by Reframing Metacognitive Interpretation of Task Difficulty," *Journal of Experimental Psychology: General* 141, no. 4 (2012): 610–618, DOI: 10.1037/a0027478.

xxxvii Lisa Firestone, "The Abuse of Overparenting," *Psychology Today*, Apr. 2, 2012, https://www.psychologytoday.com/us/blog/compassion-matters/201204/the-abuse-overparenting.

xxxviii *Critical Role*, season 4, episode 10, "Those Who Walk Away," performed by Laura Bailey, Taliesin Jaffe, Matthew Mercer, Liam O'Brien, Marisha Ray, Sam Riegel, and Travis Willingham, aired Mar. 17, 2016, on Geek & Sundry, YouTube.

xxxix Ibid.

xl "Bereavement," *Psychology Today*, Mar. 6, 2018, https://www.psychologytoday.com/us/conditions/bereavement.

xli Chris Claremont, *Avengers Annual* Vol. 1, #10, New York, NY: Marvel Comics, 1981.

xlii "Coping with Loss: Bereavement and Grief," Mental Health America, accessed July 10, 2018, http://www.mentalhealthamerica.net/conditions/coping-loss-bereavement-and-grief.

xliii Chris Claremont, *Avengers Annual* Vol. 1, #10, New York, NY: Marvel Comics, 1981.

xliv Kurt Busiek, Roger Stern, *The Invincible Iron Man* Vol. 3, #18, New York, NY: Marvel Comics, 1999.

xlv Kelly Sue DeConnick, *Captain Marvel* Vol. 1, #1, New York, NY: Marvel Comics, 2012.

xlvi Jill Lepore, "The Surprising Origin Story of Wonder Woman," Smithsonian.com, Oct. 2014, https://www.smithsonianmag.com/arts-culture/origin-story-wonder-woman-180952710/.

xlvii Tara Well, "Compassion Is Better than Empathy," *Psychology Today*, Mar. 4, 2017, https://www.psychologytoday.com/us/blog/the-clarity/201703/compassion-is-better-empathy.

xlviii Kelly Sue DeConnick (comic book writer) in discussion with the author, August 2018.

xlix Lynette L. Craft, Frank M. Perna, "The Benefits of Exercise for the Clinically Depressed." *Primary care companion to the Journal of Clinical Psychiatry* 6, no. 3 (2004): 104-111, https://www.ncbi.nlm.nih.gov/pmc/articles/PMC474733/.

l "Adversity," Merriam-Webster.com, retrieved Aug. 1, 2018, https://www.merriam-webster.com/dictionary/adversity.

li Virginia Zarulli, Julia A. Barthold Jones, Anna Oksuzyan, Rune Lindahl-Jacobsen, Kaare Christensen, James W. Vaupel, "Women live longer than men even during severe famines and crises," *Proceedings of the National Academy of Sciences* 115, no. 4 (Jan. 2018): E832–E840, DOI:10.1073/pnas.1701535115.

lii "Gender and women's mental health," World Health Organization, 2018, http://www.who.int/mental_health/prevention/genderwomen/en/.

liii Ibid.

liv Susan Krauss Whitbourne, "Why We Feel Insecure, and How We Can Stop," *Psychology Today*, Jul. 28, 2015, https://www.psychologytoday.com/us/blog/fulfillment-any-age/201507/why-we-feel-insecure-and-how-we-can-stop.

lv Janina Scarlet, "Psychology of Batgirl," *Superhero Therapy*, Aug. 29, 2015, http://www.superhero-therapy.com/2015/08/1284/.

lvi Gail Simone, *Batgirl* #16, New York, NY: DC Comics: 2013.

lvii "Disability Statistics: Information, Charts, Graphs and Tables," Disabled-World.com, last updated Oct. 2, 2018, https://www.disabled-world.com/disability/statistics/.

lviii "Advancing Women and Girls With Disabilities," USAID, accessed Dec. 2, 2018, https://www.usaid.gov/what-we-do/gender-equality-and-womens-empowerment/women-disabilities.

lix Diala Ammar and Johnny Nohra, "The Effect of Displacement on Mental Health: Staying or Leaving?" *Journal of Depression and Anxiety* 3, no. 4 (2014), doi:10.4172/2167-1044.1000e108.

lx Stephen A. Diamond, "Who Are We Really?: C. G. Jung's 'Split Personality,'" *Psychology Today*, Jul. 29, 2010, https://www.psychologytoday.com/us/blog/evil-deeds/201007/who-are-we-really-cg-jungs-split-personality.

lxi Seth J. Gillihan, "21 Common Reactions to Trauma," *Psychology Today*, Sept. 7, 2016, https://www.psychologytoday.com/us/blog/think-act-be/201609/21-common-reactions-trauma.

lxii Mariko Tamaki, *Hulk* Vol. 1, #1, New York, NY: Marvel Comics, 2017.

lxiii Mariko Tamaki, *Hulk* Vol. 1, #2, New York, NY: Marvel Comics, 2017.

lxiv Raj Raghunathan, "How Negative Is Your Metal Chatter?" *Psychology Today*, Oct. 10, 2013, https://www.psychologytoday.com/us/blog/sapient-nature/201310/how-negative-is-your-mental-chatter?collection=164978.

lxv Todd Kashdan and Robert Biswas-Diener, "Grumpy People Get the Details Right," *The Cut*, Oct. 20, 2014, an excerpt from *The Upside of Your Dark Side*, New York: Hudson Street Press, 2014. https://www.thecut.com/2014/10/grumpy-people-get-the-details-right.html.

lxvi Sam Maggs (author) in discussion with the author, August 2018.

lxvii Rudolf E. Noble, "Depression in women," *Metabolism: Clinical and Experimental* 54, no. 5 (May 2005): 49–52, https://doi.org/10.1016/j.metabol.2005.01.014.

lxviii "Facts About Women and Trauma," American Psychological Association, accessed June 4, 2018, http://www.apa.org/advocacy/interpersonal-violence/women-trauma.aspx.

lxix Molly Reynolds, "Jessica Jones: A Devastatingly Accurate Depiction of Emotional Abuse," *Huffington Post*, April 6, 2016, https://www.huffingtonpost.com/molly-reynolds/jessica-jones-a-devastati_b_9513282.html.

lxx "Get the Facts & Figures," National Domestic Violence Hotline, accessed Aug. 1, 2018, http://www.thehotline.org/resources/statistics/.

lxxi "Dissociation and Dissociative Disorders," Mental Health America, accessed Aug. 1, 2018, http://www.mentalhealthamerica.net/conditions/dissociation-and-dissociative-disorders.

lxxii *Star Trek: Voyager*, season 5, episode 3, "Extreme Risk," directed by Cliff Bole, aired Oct. 28, 1998, on United Paramount Network.

lxxiii *Star Trek: Voyager*, season 7, episode 12, "Lineage," directed by Peter Lauritson, aired Jan. 24, 2001, on United Paramount Network.

lxxiv Susan Krauss Whitbourne, "The Definitive Guide to Guilt," *Psychology Today*, Aug. 11, 2012, https://www.psychologytoday.com/us/blog/fulfillment-any-age/201208/the-definitive-guide-guilt.

lxxv "Self-Harm," National Alliance on Mental Illness, accessed Aug. 1, 2018, https://www.nami.org/Learn-More/Mental-Health-Conditions/Related-Conditions/Self-harm.

lxxvi "Depression: What You Need to Know," National Institute of Mental Health, 2015, https://www.nimh.nih.gov/health/publications/depression-what-you-need-to-know/index.shtml.

lxxvii "Depression," Mental Health America, accessed Nov. 28, 2018, http://www.mentalhealthamerica.net/conditions/depression.

lxxviii Robert Bernstein, Action Comics Vol. 1, #252, New York: DC Comics, 1959.

lxxix Alice Boyes, "Why Stress Turns Into Depression," Psychology Today, Mar. 7, 2013, https://www.psychologytoday.com/us/blog/in-practice/201303/why-stress-turns-depression.

lxxx Supergirl, season 1, episode 16, "Falling," directed by Larry Teng, aired March 14, 2016, on CW Network.

lxxxi Alice G. Walton, "Depression Isn't Always What You Think: The Subtle Signs," Forbes, Feb. 15, 2015, https://www.forbes.com/sites/alicegwalton/2015/02/17/the-subtle-symptoms-of-depression/#2781ec0f1a3e.

lxxxii Bethel Moges and Kristi Weber, "Parental Influence on the Emotional Development of Children," Developmental Psychology at Vanderbilt, May 7, 2014, https://my.vanderbilt.edu/developmentalpsychologyblog/2014/05/parental-influence-on-the-emotional-development-of-children/.

lxxxiii Stan Lee, The X-Men Vol. 1, #4, New York, NY: Marvel Comics, 1964.

lxxxiv Steve Englehart, Giant-size Avengers Vol. 1, #4, New York, NY: Marvel Comics, 1974.

lxxxv James Robinson, Scarlet Witch Vol. 2: World of Witchcraft, New York, NY: Marvel Comics: Jan. 13, 2016.

lxxxvi "Adjustment Disorder," Psychology Today, Mar. 5, 2018. https://www.psychologytoday.com/us/conditions/adjustment-disorder.

lxxxvii Ibid.

lxxxviii Lisa Aronson Fontes, "When Relationship Abuse Is Hard to Recognize," Psychology Today, Aug. 26, 2015, https://www.psychologytoday.com/us/blog/invisible-chains/201508/when-relationship-abuse-is-hard-recognize.

lxxxix Catrina Dennis (writer, host) in discussion with the author, July 2018.

xc Charlotte S. Yeh, "The power and prevalence of loneliness," *Harvard Health Blog*, Jan. 13, 2017, https://www.health.harvard.edu/blog/the-power-and-prevalence-of-loneliness-2017011310977.

xci Vito Zepinic, "Disintegration of the Self-Structure Caused by Severe Trauma," *Psychology and Behavioral Sciences* 5, no. 4 (2016): 83–92, doi:10.11648/j.pbs.20160504.12.

xcii David Spiegel, "Coming Apart: Trauma and the Fragmentation of the Self," Dana Foundation, Jan. 31, 2008, http://www.dana.org/Cerebrum/2008/Coming_Apart__Trauma_and_the_Fragmentation_of_the_Self/.

xciii eLife, "Females react differently than males to social isolation." *ScienceDaily*. Oct. 11, 2016, www.sciencedaily.com/releases/2016/10/161011125959.htm.

xciv Burgess, Lana. "What You Need To Know About Autophobia," *Medical News Today*, last updated Oct. 27, 2017, https://www.medicalnewstoday.com/articles/319816.php.

xcv Nancy Sherman, "The Moral Logic of Survivor's Guilt." *The New York Times*, Jul. 3, 2011, https://opinionator.blogs.nytimes.com/2011/07/03/war-and-the-moral-logic-of-survivor-guilt/.

xcvi "How To Deal With Survivor's Guilt," Sylvia Brafman Mental Health Center *Depression & Mental Health Blog*, accessed Nov. 25, 2018, http://mentalhealthcenter.org/how-to-deal-with-survivors-guilt/.

xcvii Alexandria Neonakis, "Game Theory: The Last Of Us, Revisited," *The New York Times*, Dec. 30, 2013, https://artsbeat.blogs.nytimes.com/2013/12/30/game-theory-the-last-of-us-revisited/.

xcviii Christopher Bergland, "*Parental Warmth Is Crucial to a Child's Well-being*," *Psychology Today*, Oct. 4, 2013, https://www.psychologytoday.com/us/blog/the-athletes-way/201310/parental-warmth-is-crucial-child-s-well-being.

xcix Ibid.

c Jefferson M. Fish, "Arranged Marriages," *Psychology Today*, Apr. 27, 2010, https://www.psychologytoday.com/us/blog/looking-in-the-cultural-mirror/201004/arranged-marriages.

ci   Catherine Pearson, "Child Marriage is 'a Major Psychological Trauma',
      New Study Says," *Huffington Post*, updated Oct. 30, 2011, https://
      www.huffingtonpost.com/2011/08/30/child-marriage-psychological-
      effects_n_941958.html.

cii   Susan Krauss Whitbourne, "The Essential Guide to Defense Mechanisms,"
      Psychology Today, Oct. 22, 2011, https://www.psychologytoday.com/
      us/blog/fulfillment-any-age/201110/the-essential-guide-defense-
      mechanisms.

ciii Frank T. McAndrew, "The Perils of Social Isolation," *Psychology Today*,
      Nov. 12, 2016, https://www.psychologytoday.com/us/blog/out-the-
      ooze/201611/the-perils-social-isolation.

civ   Dhruv Khullar, "How Social Isolation Is Killing Us," *The New York Times*,
      Dec. 22, 2016, https://www.nytimes.com/2016/12/22/upshot/how-social-
      isolation-is-killing-us.html.

cv   Ibid.

cvi   Mike Carey, *X-Men: Legacy* Vol. 1, #224, New York, NY: Marvel Comics,
      2009.

cvii Athena Chan, "Research Finds How Long-Term Social Isolation Changes
      the Brain," *Tech Times*, May 21, 2018, https://www.techtimes.com/
      articles/228082/20180521/research-finds-how-long-term-social-isolation-
      changes-the-brain.htm.

cviii Mikhail Lyubansky, "Buffy's Search for Meaning," in *The Psychology of Joss
      Whedon: An Unauthorized Exploration of Buffy, Angel, and Firefly*, ed. Joy
      Davidson (Dallas, TX: BenBella Books, Inc., 2007), 171–184.

cix   *Buffy the Vampire Slayer*, season 5, episode 22, "The Gift," directed by Joss
      Whedon, aired May 22, 2001, on WB Television Network.

cx   Mikhail Lyubansky, "Buffy's Search for Meaning," in *The Psychology of Joss
      Whedon: An Unauthorized Exploration of Buffy, Angel, and Firefly*, ed. Joy
      Davidson (Dallas, TX: BenBella Books, Inc., 2007), 171–184.

cxi   *Buffy the Vampire Slayer*, season 5, episode 22, "The Gift," directed by Joss
      Whedon, aired May 22, 2001, on WB Television Network.

cxii Sumalee Montano (actress) in discussion with the author, August 2018.

cxiii *Buffy the Vampire Slayer*, season 7, episode 22, "Chosen," directed by Joss
      Whedon, aired May 20, 2003, on United Paramount Network.

INDEX